THE UNSUNG HERO OF BIRDSONG, ~USA~

THE UNSUNG HERO OF BIRDSONG, —USA—

BRENDA WOODS

SCHOLASTIC INC.

No part of this publication may be reproduced, stored in a retrieval system, or transmitted in any form or by any means, electronic, mechanical, photocopying, recording, or otherwise, without written permission of the publisher. For information regarding permission, write to Nancy Paulsen Books, an imprint of Penguin Young Readers Group, a division of Penguin Random House LLC, 1745 Broadway, New York, NY 10019.

ISBN 978-1-338-66133-0

12 11 10 9 8 7 6 5 4 3 2 1   20 21 22 23 24 25

Printed in the U.S.A.   40

First Scholastic printing, January 2020

Design by Eileen Savage
Text set in Carre Noir

Dedicated to the memory of the heroic men
of the 761st Tank Battalion

Depth of friendship does not depend on length
of acquaintance.

—Rabindranath Tagore

CHAPTER 1

One funny thing about life and all the stuff that happens while you're living it is that mostly you only see it through your own eyes, that is, unless you decide to try to see things through the eyes of someone else. Then, you have four eyes, and looking at things with more eyes than just your own lets you see things more clearly—maybe even see things the way they really are, not just the way you want them to be.

That's what Meriwether claimed, and now I know he sure was right. But then again, seems like Meriwether was right about a whole mess of stuff.

My name is Gabriel, like the angel, but I'm sure not

ready for heaven. I don't have any brothers or sisters, and at times I wish I did. And we aren't rich, but we're a ways from being poor, and being a ways from being poor is how I got the bicycle, and having the bicycle is how I met Meriwether, and meeting Meriwether is how I learned that seeing life through more eyes than just the two on my face can make some things a lot easier to understand.

It was 1946, just another quiet Sunday in summertime, when I met him in a town not too far off from Charleston, South Carolina—a town named Birdsong. I'd just turned twelve.

CHAPTER 2

"Hot diggity dog!"

It was a brand-spanking-new Schwinn Autocycle
Deluxe with a built-in electric light—a present for my
birthday. I couldn't stop grinning. I tested the brakes,
traced the handlebars and frame with my fingers, and ran
my hand across the seat.

"Gabriel Haberlin, stop pettin' that bicycle like it's a
puppy dog," Mama said with a smile. In one hand, she
held the dirt-stained gardening gloves she wore when she
tended the vegetables in what, even though World War
II had been over for nearly a year, she still called her victory garden. The other hand reached up, brushed her long

blond hair out of her face, and tucked it behind her ears. Daddy curled his tanned, freckled arm around her shoulder. They were like a real pretty photograph right then, my mama, Agatha, and my daddy, Jake, and I wished we had a roll of film for our camera so I could take a picture of them and some of my new bicycle, but we didn't. Mama tended to be forgetful about things like that.

"Go on and take it for a ride, Gabriel," Daddy encouraged me.

So I popped up the kickstand and climbed on—all the while admiring the bright blue and white color and the perfect chrome gleaming in the sun. "Can I go show Patrick? He won't believe it 'less he sees it." Patrick's my best friend and lives across town.

"Sure, but you be careful, now," Daddy warned as he gave the back of the bike a gentle push. Sunday was his only day off, and the newspaper, which I knew he couldn't wait to get back to reading, was tucked under his arm.

"I will," I promised, and off I pedaled, glancing back once at my parents' happy faces.

"You be sure and be home way b'fore supper!" Mama hollered. "Pineapple upside-down cake you asked for is in the oven! And Cousin Polly and Them are comin' from Charleston!"

Cousin Polly is Daddy's first cousin, which I've been told makes her my first cousin once removed, and Them includes her husband, Teddy Waldrop, and their sixteen-year-old daughter, Tink, whose real name is Theodora but most people never call her that because if they do, Tink can be counted on to blow at least one fuse, sometimes more. Them also includes Teddy's mama, Auntie Rita, who claims to possess heavenly insight, meaning she has a deep understanding of spiritual things, but Mama and especially Cousin Polly don't always seem to believe her.

The fact that they were visiting today had me feeling extremely happy, because whenever Cousin Polly and Them barrel through our front door, the usually quiet house comes alive with joking and laughing, and Cousin Polly always turns the music up loud. And now I was doubly happy my cousin Tink was coming, because Tink and her two-toned green Kodak camera are like macaroni and cheese—almost always together. That she'd take more than a few pictures of me posed and smiling with my new bicycle was a sure thing, and that would make it a cinch for me to remember this day for the rest of my life.

"And tell Patrick he's welcome for cake and ice cream!" Mama added.

"Yes ma'am, I will!" I shouted.

It was so hot, it almost felt like the sun was sitting right on top of me, but as I raced, the air cooled me off. Soon, I was flying downhill, soaring like a swallow-tailed kite bird, speeding so fast I didn't even have to pedal. I glanced up, wondering if this was anything close to what my uncle Earl felt like when he was in his P-51 Mustang way up there in the sky. Now and then, I pictured myself becoming a pilot just like him.

Twelve is still kind of a baby age, I caught myself thinking as I rode along. Thirteen sure sounds two tons better. And then I almost laughed. Here I was just turning twelve and already wishing I'd crossed the finish line so I could start thirteen.

Auntie Rita has told everyone over and over since I was a little boy, "Gabriel's got the eyes of an old soul." And just that morning I'd studied my face in the mirror, searching for whatever it is Auntie Rita sees when she stares into my eyes. The way she says it, in that whispery voice of hers, makes it sound like being an old soul is a good thing. Right then, I wondered, If I am one, how exactly did that come to be, an old soul in a young body? But when the spooky Spanish moss that sways from the branches of the old oak trees that line some of Birdsong's streets tickled my face, I laughed out loud and stopped thinking about all that.

Birdsong, South Carolina, is a mostly ordinary place. The closest real city is Charleston, and one trip there is all it takes to make you understand the difference between a real city and our town. Even so, we don't drive the seventy-five miles to Charleston very often, because Birdsong, USA, has pretty much everything we need.

Main Street has a market, a post office, and a string of shops, including a five-and-dime. Plus, there's Mr. Summerlin's drugstore, which also has a soda fountain, and we even have a movie theater. Each end of town has a gas station—including one that has a garage for repairing automobiles plus a lot for selling cars that is owned and operated by my daddy, Jake Haberlin.

Mama called Birdsong a peaceful, pretty place, and most folks, including me, agreed with her.

But some things in the town of Birdsong, USA, were about to change.

CHAPTER 3

Certain things should never ever happen, especially on your birthday when you're riding your new bicycle for the first time down Main Street. And you're so busy showing off and watching people turn their heads to take notice of you that you're not paying attention to the stoplight ahead that has just turned red.

Then suddenly, from the corner of your eye, you catch a glimpse of a car in the intersection heading straight at you—the yellow Buick Roadmaster Mr. Babcock bought from Daddy for his wife, Betty, just the other day. And suddenly you realize you don't have time to swerve out of its way—so for an instant you figure you're definitely about to enter the pearly gates of heaven. And the only words that come out of your mouth are "Holy moly!"

Certain things like that should never happen. But they did.

THEN, IN A flash, you get extremely lucky. Someone pushes you out of the way so that you and the big yellow car don't collide, but instead you take a very bad dive and wind up crumpled on the street.

The first thing I saw when I opened my eyes was a sign.

Need Work
Honest
Good at fixing things

The next thing I saw was the face of the man who had the sign hanging around his neck. He was colored, and he looked sort of familiar.

"You okay?" he asked.

I sat up and shrugged. "Dunno. Think so." One of my elbows was skinned and bleeding a little. He reached down to help me up.

"Thank you, mister," I said, and tried to stand.

"Careful, now . . . Could be something broken," the man warned.

"You the one who saved me?" I asked.

"I suppose you could say that," he replied with a slight nod of his head.

"Thank you," I told him. "Thank you a lot, mister."

Once I was standing, I could see my prized possession—the car had missed me but not my Schwinn Autocycle Deluxe. The handlebars were twisted, some spokes were bent, and the light was dangling loose.

"Not too bad," he said, following my eyes. "I can fix it for you if you like. Shouldn't take but a few minutes. Got my tools right here."

I read the sign around his neck again. "I don't have nuthin' but a dime, mister," I told him.

He grinned and replied, "Save your money, young man."

Right then a woman hollering words you usually only hear in church interrupted us. "Oh, my Jesus! Lord have mercy on my soul!"

It was Betty Babcock. She had stumbled out of her car in her high-heeled shoes and was quickly making her way over to me. Other people joined her, and soon, like pigeons pecking at a handful of tossed bread crumbs, they formed a huddle around me.

"I'm fine as could be," I told them.

The red-faced butcher from DeVear's grocery store slipped his arms around me and practically carried me over to the curb. The gawking audience trailed us, questions flying from their mouths.

"Are you dizzy?"

I sat down. "No."

"Can you see?"

"Better than a hawk."

"Is anything broken?"

I'm not Superman with X-ray vision, I wanted to reply but didn't. Besides, from what Patrick had told me about how bad it hurt when he fell off his roof and cracked his arm bone in two, I figured nothing was broken. "Don't think so," I answered.

Then Mrs. Babcock started yelling again. "My light was green! Tell 'em it was green, Gabriel Haberlin! Tell 'em, please!" Her hair, which Cousin Polly and Auntie Rita claim is not a gift from God but comes instead from her Charleston hairdresser, looked like a bright yellow bird's nest.

"It's true," I told them. "I wasn't payin' attention. It's not her fault . . . not at all. Plus, I'm truly fine as could be."

That was when Mrs. Betty Babcock got down on

her knees in the middle of Main Street, closed her eyes, reached up toward heaven, and shouted three times in a row, "Hallelujah and thank you, Lord!"

It was then I noticed Rosie Riley in the crowd. Rosie is one of the nicest girls at school, and when she laughs, it's loud and not pretend. She's a year older than me and is the eldest child of Howard Riley, MD, and claims she is going to be a doctor just like him.

Concern was swimming in her eyes. "Are you all right, Gabriel?" she asked. "Maybe I should go get my daddy."

Having her attention made me grin. "You kiddin'? It'd take more than this to damage my armor." I bent my elbow and flexed my muscle, producing a small bulge. "See?"

A smile parted her lips. "Good," Rosie Riley replied.

Faces that had previously been full of distress now appeared relieved, and I heard a few snickers.

"I'm fine," I repeated. "Plus, today's my birthday."

Birthday wishes spouted quickly from here and there, but only Rosie's words sounded like a song.

"Happy birthday, Gabriel. I'm glad you weren't hurt. Woulda been a shame for you to get smashed up bad, especially on your birthday. See ya," Rosie said, and then she turned and walked away. As usual, my eyes couldn't help but follow her. She was wearing blue plaid shorts and penny loafers without socks, but I zeroed in on the dance of her straw-colored ponytail as she pranced off.

And knowing that Rosie Riley was glad I hadn't bitten the dust made me grin some more.

CHAPTER 4

Mr. Summerlin, the gray-haired owner of the drug-store and soda fountain, patted the top of my head. "You're a lucky boy, Gabriel . . . mighty lucky indeed," he declared. "Must be a guardian angel watchin' over you."

"Angel? It wasn't an angel. It was a man who saved me," I told him.

"What man?" a handful of people asked at the same time.

I scanned the faces around me, but his wasn't among them. Then I looked beyond the crowd and saw him standing across the street with his tools, fixing my bicycle.

I pointed. "Him. He pushed me out of the way just in time."

One by one heads quickly turned, until finally all eyes were on the man who'd likely saved my life.

"Meriwether?" Mr. Summerlin asked.

"That his name?" I asked.

"Yes. Mighty good at fixing things. Does work for me now and then at the store," he replied.

"He sure kept you from buyin' the farm, huh?" the butcher commented.

"Yessir," I replied. "I thought for sure I was a goner."

And then, I guess because most people could see I wasn't mangled and others couldn't wait to go wag their tongues about my brush with death, the crowd began to vanish until there were only three left: Mr. Summerlin, Mrs. Babcock, and Miss Felicity Duval, who plays the organ at church and gives piano lessons for a dime out of her house.

"I should call your mama 'n' daddy . . . have 'em let Doc Riley give you the once-over . . . just in case, especially that elbow," Mr. Summerlin advised.

"Please don't do that! I'm fine." I gazed at my new possession. "Pleeeze, Mr. Summerlin . . . They'll take my bicycle away and I'll never be able to ride it again. I'll be more careful. I promise. It's my birthday . . . Pleeeze!" I begged.

Mr. Summerlin sighed. "Just doesn't feel right . . . your folks not knowin'," he said, and then he looked at Miss Duval, as if seeking her opinion.

She reached into her purse, took out a fancy kerchief, and wiped sweat from her forehead before nodding in agreement.

Miss Duval then turned to Mrs. Betty Babcock, who said, "Wouldn't surprise me if they already know."

As if thinking that Mrs. Babcock was probably right, the three of them snatched looks at one another and grinned.

"Y'all have a lovely Sunday," Miss Duval told Mrs. Babcock and Mr. Summerlin, and then she turned her attention to me. "And Gabriel?"

"Yes ma'am?"

"Please be more cautious. Might not be anyone there to save you the next time you choose to be careless with your life."

"Won't be a next time, Miss Duval," I informed her.

"Good to hear. Have a good day," she said, and

strutted off in that way she does, heels clicking, head held high.

And that was when the man who had saved my life strolled toward us, guiding the bicycle. He and Mr. Summerlin greeted each other politely, but Mrs. Babcock stared off down the street, as if the man were invisible, the way some white ladies do when there's a colored man close by.

"'Bout good as new as I could get it, young man," he said.

I checked it over from end to end. He'd even fixed the light.

"Holy mackerel!" I exclaimed. "It really is good as new! Thank you, Mr. . . ." I'm never too good at remembering names, and with everything that had happened, I'd forgotten his in a flash.

"Hunter, Meriwether Hunter," he replied. His short wiry hair was black, and his skin was dark brown. He had a nice smile and a thick mustache and was tall, but not so tall that a person would think too much about it.

I introduced myself. "I'm Gabriel."

"It's a fine name," he replied.

I read the sign around his neck again.

"Can you fix cars?" I asked.

"Most things with an engine."

"Even a P-51 Mustang?" I inquired.

"A fighter plane? Never worked on one, but I suppose an engine's an engine."

"My uncle Earl was a pilot, flew a P-51 in the war. He was even at the Battle of the Bulge," I boasted.

He looked away before replying, "That so . . . Battle of the Bulge?"

"Yeah, but not long after that, he got hurt . . . Broke some bones when he crash-landed, but they were able to fix him so he's almost good as new."

"Kinda like your bicycle," he said.

"Yessir, I spoze so," I answered, then continued, "He's a gen-u-wine war hero, and soon as I'm of age, I'm gonna enlist and go to flight school too. He'll be in Charleston on Saturday. They're havin' a big parade for all of the South Carolina war heroes," I informed him.

He looked up at the sky, squinted into the sun, then gazed off toward the green foothills. "A parade" was all he said.

Mr. Summerlin finally cut in, "'Bout time I headed back to work—and Meriwether?"

"Sir?"

"Thank you . . . for preventin' this from becomin' a very tragic day."

"You're mighty welcome, Mr. Summerlin, sir," he replied.

"Gabriel?" Mrs. Babcock interrupted.

"Yes ma'am."

"Hurt or not, I'd like to see to it that you get home safe and sound."

"But I was 'bouta go show Patrick . . ."

She didn't let me finish. Instead, she spoke to Meriwether. "Do you think the bicycle will fit in my car, boy?"

Meriwether's eyes met the ground. "In a big ole Roadmaster? It sure oughtta, ma'am."

"But . . ." I pleaded.

"But nuthin', Gabriel Haberlin. I've decided," she replied softly, but there was steel mixed in with her words, like Mama's words get when there's no changing her mind, so I knew Betty Babcock meant it. "Put the bicycle in the car," she commanded Meriwether.

"Thank you again, sir," I told him.

"Welcome," he replied.

And just like that, I was sitting next to Betty Babcock. While she started the car, I swiveled and peered out the back window. Mr. Meriwether Hunter stood there alone on the sidewalk, frozen like something carved out of stone, the Need Work sign still around his neck.

Mrs. Babcock gently patted my hand and put her foot on the gas, and the big yellow chariot zoomed down the street.

CHAPTER 5

I didn't know if Betty Babcock was bad at anything else, but it took me less than a minute to figure out that she was really bad at driving. In fact, Betty Babcock was such a dreadfully rotten driver that I was curious about how she'd ever passed a driving test. Less than half an hour earlier, she'd nearly killed me, so you'd think that would have made her drive cautiously, but no—instead she sped, swerving and careering around corners like she was behind the wheel of a race car at the Indianapolis Motor Speedway.

When she screeched to an abrupt stop at a stop sign, I actually smelled burnt tire rubber. The car hadn't even come to a complete stop when she put her foot on the gas and sped off again.

"Aren't you spozed to actually stop and look both ways?" I asked.

"Oh shush! You sound just like that pesky man at the motor vehicle place . . . the one who gave me my driver's test. I'm an excellent driver. Got good instincts."

That started me giggling.

She took her eyes off the road and gave me a look. But then her lead foot eased up and she began to drive at a normal speed, causing me to let out an extremely long sigh of relief.

I stared out at the countryside the rest of the ride home and started wondering exactly who might be calling my parents right now—Mr. Summerlin or the butcher or Miss Duval or someone else? Knowing how fast news travels in this small town, I could be certain someone had.

When Mrs. Babcock pulled the car to a stop in front of my house, I quickly climbed out. Made it, I thought.

And right then, Cousin Polly and Them pulled up behind Mrs. Babcock. Their black Ford was sputtering the way it always does, and their hands were waving and their faces were smiling.

I was about to wave back, but I didn't have time to

because Mama had come running out of the house and wrapped her arms around me. "Gabriel!" she yelled.

Tink climbed out of their car, pointed her camera at us, and snapped a photo. It wasn't the first picture I'd daydreamed about her taking of me today, but it was definitely part of this day's story.

My assumption that someone had squealed and filled Mama and Daddy's ears with news of my mishap was now a crystal-clear certainty. Daddy stood in front of me, and I could tell he didn't know which path to take, the thankful or angry one. I was happy when thankful won. His eyes got watery, and he patted my head. Mama finally released me and wiped at her tears.

Tink looked out from behind her camera. "What's buzzin', cuzzin?" she asked me.

Mrs. Babcock, who had joined us on the sidewalk, answered for me. "What's buzzin' is that Gabriel was being careless as he rode his bicycle down Main Street and sailed through a red light, but I am happy to say that my excellent driving skills allowed me to avoid a tragic accident. So here he is, alive and well, safe and sound."

"But Mrs. Babcock . . . that man, Mr. Meriwether, he pushed me out of the way just in time. Wasn't for him, I might have got killed."

"Well . . . that too. Yes."

"That's exactly what Miss Duval told us," Mama informed her.

So, Miss Duval—who everyone claimed was a speedier carrier of news than the *Birdsong Gazette*—had been the informant.

Minutes later, the bicycle was out of the car and Mrs. Babcock had been thanked. Daddy shook her hand, and Mama even hugged her.

If you knew what a terrible driver she is, I don't think you'd be so grateful, I thought. Boy, I couldn't wait to spill the beans on her. But the shocked looks Mama, Daddy, Cousin Polly, and Them passed around when Mrs. Babcock screeched off in her Roadmaster made me figure they wouldn't require much convincing.

To my surprise, Daddy handed off the bicycle to me, and together we all strode to the front porch.

"Swanky cycle, Gabriel," Tink commented.

"Yeah, it's really swell, and boy, does it fly," I told her.

"Attention! Everyone halt!" Tink suddenly ordered. "I wanna take a picture."

Her father, Teddy, chuckled. "And what else is new?"

As directed, we stood together and posed.

Tink pointed her camera and focused. "This is a special day we should always remember."

"Yes 'tis . . . Gabriel's birthday number twelve," Auntie Rita replied.

"But it's even more special than a birthday," Tink said. She had a sly grin on her face.

"Why's that?" Cousin Polly asked.

Tink snapped the picture. "Because his birthday almost became his death day."

Tears returned to Mama's eyes, and she squeezed Daddy's hand and my shoulder.

"Tink! How can you be so crass?" Cousin Polly hollered.

"Jeepers creepers! It was just a joke," she replied.

Auntie Rita shook her head. "Tsk, tsk, tsk . . . Death ain't sumthin' to poke fun at, Theodora."

At the sound of her real name, Tink frowned.

"Apologize to Gabriel this instant!" Cousin Polly insisted.

"I'm sorry, Gabriel."

"Thank you, The-o-dora."

Tink sneered, "Rub it in deep, why don't you?"

I smirked and replied, "I just did."

Daddy interrupted the silliness. "Gabriel, put the bicycle in the shed. We'll talk about what we are going to do with it later." He had his no-nonsense look.

So I gave him my no-nonsense answer. "Yessir."

The look in his eyes gave me a clue about what was coming. And from what I surmised, the bicycle might not be part of my future.

CHAPTER 6

"You know, I'm really happy you didn't croak, Gabriel. And I didn't mean to make everyone flip their wigs," Tink said, tagging along as I walked my bike to the shed.

"Flip their wigs?" I asked.

Tink interpreted, "Get upset."

More and more, since a girl named Helene from New York City had moved in next door to Tink and become her best friend, Tink had started using what Daddy refers to as *modern lingo*. But recently, because Helene was making Tink see things in a whole different way, more than Tink's words were new. Just last month, when they'd come to visit, the two of us were walking to the movie theater when she'd stopped abruptly in front of a store called Lolly's Antiques. Tink's eyes had focused on the whites-only sign in the window, and my cousin had frowned. "Can you imagine bein' colored and havin' to put up with this injustice?" Tink asked me. "Helene says they don't have such signs in New York City."

Of course, Tink had snapped a picture of the sign, and when I asked her why, she'd told me she was preserving history. "Because according to Helene's father, who is a professor of American history, whites and coloreds won't be segregated in the South someday, and all these things he calls Jim Crow signs will be gone."

Now Tink said to me, "So, your parents are gonna wait 'til after we leave to bust your chops, right?"

"Bust my chops?"

"Yeah—yell and fuss . . . get stinkin' mad at you. And probably take the bike away."

"I spoze they will," I answered solemnly. "Can you get a bunch of pictures of me on it?"

"Sure thing, cousin. Plus, it's all good practice for when I get hired at *Life* magazine or *National Geographic*. Only then I'll be off taking pics of faraway places or indigenous people."

"What's *indigenous*?" I inquired as she posed me.

"The people who were in a country first, like the Indians were here. Or the Maya in Mexico and the Aborigines in Australia. I'm already making a portfolio of my best photographs. As soon as I graduate high school, I, Tink Waldrop, am gonna blow this place called South Carolina and travel the world. And that's not just me flappin' my lips. I'm really gonna amscray."

"You are really something else, Tink," I said, then crossed my eyes at her.

"And you, cousin, are off the cob."

This time, I wanted to pretend that I understood what she meant, but my curiosity quickly conquered my pride and I asked, "Off the cob?"

"Corny."

"Oh, I get it."

While Tink snapped away with the camera, I did my best to look as happy as I'd felt when I'd just gotten the bicycle, but it was hard. When she was finished, I parked it in a corner inside the shed and stared at it for a while. "I'm just a pigheaded lamebrain. I can't blame anyone but myself. I should have been payin' attention." I didn't want to cry, but sadness had already sent its message to my eyes.

"Dry your peepers and stop your snivelin', Gabriel,"

Tink told me, "because I'm in the know about this kind of thing."

"Okay, snivelin' stopped. Now explain what you're talkin' about."

"I'm gonna give you some advice that just might help you keep your bicycle."

"Give."

"First—and this is real important—admit you were wrong. Then, tell them you're so very sorry because you know how much they love you and how upset they must be. Plus, promise that you'll be extremely careful from now on. Finally, try your best to look sad all day—but especially through dinner, even when you open your presents and see the candles on the birthday cake. When everyone tells you to make a wish before you blow out the candles, fold your hands and close your eyes like you're prayin'. Make 'em feel sorry for you. It's a good formula but not foolproof, meanin' there's a chance it won't work."

"And if it doesn't?"

"Hmm? Can't say, but it oughtta be duck soup."

The rest of the day reminded me of warm saltwater taffy—easily stretched out, very sticky but tasting good.

Obeying Tink's rules was the sticky part, making me feel like a circus performer walking a tightrope, trying hard not to lose my balance. Whenever I faltered on my invisible high wire by kidding around, a warning glare from Tink was all it took to keep me from falling. The tasting-good part was how Cousin Polly and Them usually make me feel—same as beams of sunshine sneaking through clouds on a rainy day. And the stretched-out part was the way the minutes were pretending to be hours, until I finally figured this was only because I was anticipating the verdict about the bicycle that would be given at the end of the day.

CHAPTER 7

When Cousin Polly, Mama, and Auntie Rita headed off to the kitchen to get dinner ready, Daddy began belly-aching to Teddy about how one of his two mechanics had quit without any warning.

"No warnin' at all?" Teddy asked.

"None whatsoever. Found him a lady friend up in Raleigh and he was gone like the wind. Most beautiful woman he ever laid eyes on is how he tells it."

Teddy grinned. "Can't blame him for that, now, can we?"

Daddy laughed and shook his head.

The smells coming from the kitchen were making my mouth water. Finally the kitchen door swung open, and in no time flat, the table was loaded with steaming food. Roast beef, mashed potatoes and gravy, green beans, corn that had been shaved from the cob, biscuits dripping with butter and honey, and a pitcher full of lemonade crowded the table. Teddy nearly knocked over the pitcher as he reached across for the potatoes.

"As y'all can see, we clearly need a larger table," Mama said, and everyone agreed but I accidentally smiled, causing Tink to nudge my leg under the table and shoot me a look that said Cut it out, which in turn led Auntie Rita to take notice.

"What have you two cooked up?" she asked, searching our faces for clues.

"Nuthin's cookin', Grand-ma-ma," Tink replied.

"And stop callin' me Grand-ma-ma. Call me Nana like you always have."

Cousin Polly joined in the conversation. "Until Miss Helen-with-an-E Reynolds from New York City arrived next door."

"Her name's Helene, not Helen-with-an-E, and not only is she intelligent and enlightened, but she's also a gas," Tink told us. "A total gas."

Cousin Polly clicked her tongue. "Fulla gas is what I call it."

Chuckles and laughter were popping up when Tink spouted off, "As usual, Mama, you are off the cob."

Cousin Polly glared at her. "That's some kinda cruel insult, ain't it? I'm 'bouta jerk a knot in your tail."

I scooped up a forkful of corn and interpreted, "It just means corny."

Teddy patted his wife's hand. "See, Polly . . . Don't have a hissy. And Tink?"

"Yes, Daddy."

"Even if you don't . . . can you at least pretend you have some breedin'?"

Changing the subject was something Auntie Rita was known for, and that's exactly what she did. She cleared her throat twice and asked me, "Gabriel, were you aware that to have been saved the way you were today means you likely have a special destiny?"

"No ma'am, I wasn't."

"And for a total stranger to risk his life to save yours . . . My oh my, ain't that somethin' that surely leaves a sweet taste inside you?"

I nodded.

"I've heard tell that when someone saves your life, a special bond is created 'tween you and it's likely you'll be indebted to him."

"So, I owe him?" I asked.

"Indeed," she replied.

"What'd you say his name was?" Daddy asked.

"Meriwether," I responded.

At the mention of the name, Teddy's face lit up. "Fine name, Meriwether. Meriwether Lewis was the soldier and explorer who headed the Lewis and Clark Expedition back in the 1800s and reached the Pacific Ocean in—?" Teddy searched his memory for the answer and found it: "1805." Teddy claims his mind is full of mostly useless facts, but Auntie Rita proudly boasts that her son's so smart, he ought to be a contestant on the radio show *Twenty Questions.*

"I learned about Lewis and Clark in history class, but first names didn't get talked about, at least I don't think they did," I told him.

"Don't care much about what his name is . . . Mighty glad he happened to be there is all," Mama said, her eyes brimming with tears again.

Auntie Rita patted her hand. "I am doubtful that he just happened to be there, Agatha. This was certainly divine intervention."

Cousin Polly rolled her eyes.

But Auntie Rita, who usually doesn't miss a thing,

caught a glimpse of Polly's shenanigans and slyly re-marked, "Well, bless your heart, Polly Waldrop, ain't you precious." It didn't sound like an insult but it was. "I'm fixin' to delve into somethin' of spiritual importance. Is that all right with you, dear?"

Polly's face looked the way Mama's does when she pricks herself accidentally with a sewing needle. "I reckon."

"Now then, look at me, Gabriel, and try not to blink," Rita ordered.

"Yes ma'am."

As usual, she stared deeply into my eyes, and I won-dered if the old soul was still in there and, if it was, could she see him, and if she could see him, exactly how old he was. But this time she peered for so long that I got fidgety, because it seemed like she was tinkering around inside my thoughts.

Finally, she looked away through the open window and up toward the sky. "Yes, my boy with the old soul . . . you most surely have a special destiny."

"Special destiny?" I asked.

"Perhaps you'll have a lifetime fulla exceptional good works or achieve something of remarkable significance during your earthly time. A special destiny should never be interfered with by no one, no way, no how."

Suddenly, I felt as if I'd stepped into a moonlit swamp. I shivered.

Tink noticed. "Stoppit, Nana . . . You're givin' him the willies."

But Auntie Rita continued, "And I hope y'all can appreciate that it certainly wasn't meant to be . . . for the very automobile sold by the daddy . . . to take the life of his child."

To me, that sounded like she was blaming Daddy, so I sprang to my feet. "He's not the one to blame! It was my fault for not being careful . . . all mine! Well, maybe some of it belongs to Mr. Babcock for buyin' a car for his wife, who is the rottenest driver in all of Birdsong . . . probably the worst driver in all of Carolina, North and South. And I bet Daddy didn't even know about that . . . so you can't blame him, Auntie Rita, you can't blame Daddy for nuthin'!"

Auntie Rita calmly replied, "Not puttin' blame on your daddy, Gabriel. Just sayin' you clearly weren't meant to be harmed by a car your daddy sold."

Daddy took a deep breath. "All right now, Rita." Which I took to mean that it was time for her to be quiet.

Auntie Rita didn't take the hint and started up again. "And one more thing—"

But Teddy cut her off and blurted, "In other words, Mama, put a button on your lip!" So she did.

Cousin Polly giggled.

Soon as supper was over, the pineapple upside-down cake was placed on the table and the twelve candles were hastily lit.

"I didn't burn it this time, y'all," Mama said proudly.

As Tink had schooled me, I joined my hands together and whispered a prayer no one could hear but me: "Please, God, lemme please, please, please keep my bicycle." Then I finished with a loud "Amen," and when I looked into my parents' eyes, I thought I saw pity.

With one long breath, I blew out every candle and hoped.

CHAPTER 8

I sat between Mama and Daddy on the tan sofa in our parlor. Matching white lamps with yellow daisies painted on them rested atop identical wooden tables and cast their glow on us. Cousin Polly and Them had gone, the radio had been turned off, and the house had returned to its normal quiet state.

As I'd expected, Daddy began the questioning. "About Mrs. Babcock . . . Her light was green, wasn't it?"

"Yessir."

"And your light was red?"

"Yessir."

"So, rotten driver or not, is she to blame?"

"Nossir."

He continued to grill me. "And is Mr. Babcock even a little bit to blame for buyin' her the car?"

"Nossir, not a bit."

"Have I made my point, Gabriel?"

"Yessir, better than Perry Mason."

Mama laughed.

Then I spouted off some of the things Tink had told me to say. "I admit I was wrong, and I'm really sorry, because I know how much you love me and how upset you must be."

Except for Daddy clearing his throat, they were quiet and still.

"About the bicycle," I added, "the man fixed it almost good as new."

"Let's all go have a look at it, then," he finally said.

Together we headed to the shed and Daddy went over it from front to back. "He's right, Agatha. It's 'bout good as new."

"Yeah, he's really good at fixin' things," I said.

"Tell you what, Gabriel. I want you to bring the almost-good-as-new bicycle into the house and take it to your room."

"Why, Daddy?"

"I want you to park it there for two weeks."

"Then what?"

"Do you suppose that being forced to look at it day and night for two weeks but not being able to ride it will supply you with enough torment?"

"More than enough."

"Then that's your punishment . . . two weeks," he remarked.

Was I hearing right? "I get to keep it?"

"Yes," Mama answered, "but if we hear any tittle-tattle that you've been careless on it, it'll be gone for good, understand?"

"I understand . . . Thank you, Mama. Thank you, Daddy! You won't be sorry. I'll be extra careful from now on, I promise!"

I led the bicycle through the back door and into my bedroom and parked it next to the window. They had trailed me and stood together in the doorway, Mama's head resting on Daddy's shoulder, another pretty picture that wouldn't be taken.

"About that man named Meriwether who pushed me out of the way . . . He knows how to fix engines too, so maybe he could come work for you now that the other fella up and quit."

"Sure," Dad replied in a nonchalant way. "Happy birthday, son. G'night."

Mama came over and pecked me on the cheek. "G'night, Gabriel . . . Sleep well."

I gazed at the Schwinn Autocycle Deluxe and told them, "Thank you for letting me keep it."

"Welcome," they said at the same time.

CHAPTER 9

I was somewhere between where sleep ends and awake begins when I heard Patrick outside my bedroom window, calling my name. "Gabriel! Gabriel! Gabriel! You awake?" My eyes fluttered open.

I rolled out of bed and parted the curtains. Patrick was wearing swimming goggles and grinning. His hair was wet, and it was likely he'd already been to the pool, where he went first thing 'most every morning because he's got it in his mind to become a US Navy frogman.

"Where is it? You still got it or did they take it away?"

I knew what *it* was—the bicycle. As usual, the news

had taken less than a day to fly around the town. I motioned for him to come around to the kitchen door.

Like most mornings, the smell of coffee from the percolator filled the room.

"Mornin', Mama," I said.

"Mornin'," she replied. "That boy ever hear of a doorbell?" She smiled before answering her own question. "I guess not."

My hand was barely on the doorknob when Patrick pushed inside. He peeled off his goggles, which left round imprints around his eyes. "Mornin', Mrs. Haberlin," he said politely.

"Mornin', Patrick. Still aimin' to be a frogman, I see."

"Yes ma'am. If the United States Navy'll have me. I'll be mighty proud to serve."

"I'm sure they'll be more than proud. You hungry for some oatmeal and toast? I was fixin' to make some."

Patrick replied, "You know I never turn down a meal, Mrs. Haberlin."

As soon as Mama got to cooking, he nudged me and whispered, "Well, where is it?"

"Follow me," I replied, and Patrick was on my heels.

"A Schwinn Autocycle Deluxe," he said, reaching out

and touching it. "I cain't hardly believe it! Are they lettin' you keep it?"

I nodded yes.

"You gotta be kiddin'. After it nearly got you killed? My mama and daddy said they woulda taken a sledge-hammer to it."

"Can't ride it for two weeks, though, and it's gotta stay here in my room, where I have to see it night and day."

"May as well crucify you, huh?"

"May as well."

Soon as we'd finished breakfast and I'd done my daily chores, I announced to Mama, "Patrick and I are going to town and then by Daddy's work."

She was getting her jars ready to can some peaches. "Make sure you cross the threshold to this house before twilight."

"Yes ma'am."

"Let's go fishin'," Patrick suggested. "Get your pole."

"Naw, I got somethin' important to do," I told him. "I gotta find the man who saved my life so I can tell him about the job."

"Oh, the colored man," Patrick said.

So, I thought, that detail had been spilled too. "His

name's Meriwether . . . like Meriwether Lewis, who led the Lewis and Clark expedition," I rambled, trying to impress him with how smart I was.

"Yeah, I remember. How we gonna find him, anyway?" Patrick asked.

"Dunno. Maybe he'll be sittin' right where he was yesterday."

"What if he ain't?"

"We'll head to Mr. Summerlin's drugstore. He might know 'cause Mr. Meriwether does work for him now and then. Plus, probably not another man in town has that name. We're sure to get a lead that way. It's never that hard to find someone unless they don't want to be found, right?" I replied.

"You've had your ears tuned to a lot of detective radio shows, Gabriel."

He was right, I had.

Mr. Meriwether wasn't sitting or standing anywhere in town as far as we could see, so we made a beeline to Mr. Summerlin's place. He was waiting on a customer who was filling him in on the details of his recent gallbladder surgery and lifted his shirt to show him the scar. "Lordy be!" Mr. Summerlin declared.

I was itching to find Mr. Meriwether, and it was

hard to wait while the man went on and on. Just when I thought he'd run out of words, he'd start up again.

"Finally," I said when he left.

"No bicycle today, Gabriel?" Mr. Summerlin asked.

"Nossir, not for two whole weeks," I replied.

"Must feel like a long time to someone your age," he remarked.

"Yessir . . . but at least it's not forever."

"Yeah . . . there's no end to forever," Patrick added, but right away he asked, "Did forever even have a beginnin'?"

Mr. Summerlin looked as confused as I felt. "Hmm?" was all he said.

"About Mr. Meriwether?" I asked.

"Mr. Hunter is his name, Mr. Meriwether Hunter," he corrected me.

"I was hopin' you might know where he lives 'cuz I need to talk to him 'bout a job at my daddy's. One of his mechanics up and quit, and he, Mr. Hunter, told me he knows how to fix engines. So . . . I was figurin' they could help each other."

"That's mighty good of you, Gabriel. I don't know the exact address, but I know the street and the house because I gave him a lift home one night after he'd done some work here and it was pourin' rain. Of course, it's on

The Other Side. Holly Street near Eagle, third house from the corner, if I remember correctly . . . left-hand side of the street." Then, the way people do when a memory that was asleep suddenly wakes up, he smacked his head and started scrolling through his card file. "Filled a prescription for his wife a while back, and I always keep a record of the address and phone number if there is one. Here it is: Hunter, 127 Holly Street."

"127 Holly Street. Thanks, Mr. Summerlin."

"Yeah, thanks, Mr. Summerlin," Patrick echoed.

And we were off.

An army of clouds had gathered above, cooling off the morning, defending us from the summer sun as we walked.

Patrick fingered the chain around his neck and then displayed the silver medal that he wore day and night. "Mama said if you'da been wearin' a Saint Christopher medal like mine yesterday, it's likely none of that woulda happened. Also said she's gonna get you one next time she's in Charleston and even get it blessed by the archbishop for double protection."

"I'm not Catholic," I reminded him. "I'm Methodist."

"Don't matter . . . 'Least Mama claims it don't. Saint Christopher'll protect you anyways."

I shrugged and replied, "Okay."

"When you get your bicycle back, can I ride it sometimes?" Patrick asked.

"You betcha," I promised.

He patted my shoulder. "Two weeks ain't really that long. It'll go by in no time."

I hoped he was right.

Ahead, the railroad tracks and small grocery store right beside them let me know that we were about to cross into what most folks around Birdsong refer to as The Other Side.

I come here now and then with Mama when she drops off a lady named Mrs. Masters, who helps her with spring cleaning and serves when we have Christmas parties. Mostly colored people live here, and that includes, according to Mrs. Masters, five families of Gullah-Geechees who somehow made their way here from the Carolina Sea Islands and speak their own language.

Patrick and I strolled through The Other Side and passed a Baptist church and the colored school, which is actually just a small house. Once, just a couple of weeks earlier, when I had to bring five dollars to Mrs. Masters that Mama owed her, curiosity kept poking at me until it finally forced me to peek through the windows. A single room with a blackboard and a few rows of desks was all I saw. Right then, I'd wondered why my school has so many classrooms plus a library and a playground and a cafeteria too, when all the colored kids have is this one room. And that night after supper, I'd asked Mama and Daddy about it.

"Things are not always fair to colored folks," Daddy had told me.

"Why?"

Daddy had let out a loud sigh. "Well, Gabriel. You'll learn some people just feel the need to think they are better than other folks strictly because of the color of their skin. But I say this: treat all folks, regardless of color, with courtesy and respect. And be as good a person as you can be. Simple as that." Then, he'd buried his face in the newspaper.

I had taken this to mean that the conversation was supposed to be over, but my mind was still working. "Tink told me they don't have segregation and whites-only signs in New York City, so colored people can go wherever they please, and her friend Helene's father, who's a college professor, says one day all those signs will be gone and segregation too."

Daddy had put down the newspaper, glanced at

Mama, twisted his mouth a little—the way he sometimes does when he's trying to decide exactly what to say—then set me straight. "Truth be told, Gabriel, there may not be signs, but there are still lots of places up North where colored people aren't welcome at all and others where, even if they get their foot through the door, they're treated in a distasteful manner. I hope to God the professor is right, though, about the signs being gone someday. Be a good thing for colored people not to have constant reminders of being unwelcome. Just imagine if those signs, instead of saying No Colored Allowed, said No Whites Allowed. How'd that make you feel?"

I'd pictured a sign like that in my mind, and the feeling it had given me was different from any feeling I'd ever had before. I didn't know what to call it, but if feelings carried smells with them, the one I was having would stink about as bad as the time I'd been sprayed by a skunk.

After a while, my gaze had returned to Daddy, but his eyes had already traveled away from me and back to the newspaper, so nothing else was said.

But ever since then, when I see one of those signs here and there in Birdsong, I think of that smell and imagine the signs gone.

CHAPTER 10

"Holly Street," Patrick said, reading the street sign. "Which way?"

Following Mr. Summerlin's directions, I replied, "This way."

"Better not get us lost," Patrick said, "and don't say nuthin' 'bout us bein' over here to my daddy or mama."

"How come?"

"You know why, Gabriel . . . It's The Other Side. Don't your mama and daddy teach you?"

"Mama says white, colored, or whatever . . . on the inside we're all human beings."

"But cain't nobody see our insides, Gabriel, only the outsides." He paused, then asked, "Wonder what insides look like, anyhow."

"You sure have an interesting way of thinking," I told him.

Patrick shrugged and smiled.

The sign on the house said 127. It was white with gray trim and a yellow door. Two cars were parked in the driveway; both had their hoods popped, and one was jacked up.

Suddenly, a girl jumped from behind a tall hedge that was covered with blue morning glory flowers, nearly scaring the life out of me, and I flinched.

"What're you lookin' for?" she asked.

She was colored, with braided hair, and looked about ten years old. For someone her age, she had a big voice. "I said, what're you lookin' for, scaredy-cat?"

"This where Mr. Meriwether Hunter lives?" I inquired.

"Why do you wanna know?"

Patrick tugged my shirt. "Let's go!"

Suddenly I heard noises from underneath one of the cars and a man's voice called out, "Abigail?"

"Huh?" she replied.

"Who are you fussin' at?" the man asked.

"These two white boys, that's who. A tall one and a short one, and the tall one's a scaredy-cat!"

Sounds of tools clanking were followed by the commotion of him getting out from under the car. He stood up, and as soon as he saw me, a smile brightened his face. "Gabriel," Mr. Meriwether Hunter said. "Fine day to be alive, isn't it?"

I grinned and nodded.

Patrick tugged on my shirt again. "That him?"

"That's him."

Meriwether Hunter grabbed a rag, wiped his greasy hands, and strode toward us. The girl hurried to his side, took his hand, and asked, "You know them, Daddy?"

"Just the taller boy, Abigail. He's the one almost got hit by that car yesterday."

"Oh . . ." Her attention turned to me. "Better be glad my daddy was there when you were actin' a plum fool on that bicycle."

Patrick chuckled at that, and an embarrassed look pasted itself on the face of Mr. Meriwether Hunter.

"Plum fool," Abigail repeated.

"That's enough now," he scolded. "Gabriel's his name."

He reached out his hand, I extended mine, and we shook. "Hi, Mr. Hunter," I said.

"Was hardly expectin' to see you again so soon," he said, then glanced at Patrick. "Your friend got a name?"

"I'm Patrick . . . Patrick Kelly," he replied.

Mr. Meriwether Hunter reached out to shake his hand. Patrick glanced at me like he needed an answer to a question. I glared at him and jabbed him with my elbow. Finally, Patrick took his hand and they shook.

"Pleased to meet you, son. Very pleased indeed," Meriwether told him.

"Thank you, uncle," Patrick replied.

This was what plenty of white people in Birdsong did—instead of calling grown colored people by their names, they called the men *uncle* and the women *auntie*. Or, regardless of how old they were, colored men were called *boys* and the women called *girls*. But my mama and daddy had taught me differently. Every adult, white or colored, unless I'd been given permission to call them by their first names, was a *Mister* or *Missus* or *Miss*.

"The Haberlins are different," I'd heard some folks say about my parents. "All that time spent up there at that northern college must have caused it. Neither one's been quite the same since." Folks around town had made it sound like northern ways were a contagious disease that both my parents had caught.

My parents had met at Oberlin College in Ohio, married as soon as they'd graduated, then headed back to Carolina and settled in Daddy's hometown of Birdsong.

Meriwether gestured toward his daughter. "This is my girl, Abigail."

Greetings were spoken, but I could tell Patrick and Abigail were both leery.

"Well, unless y'all have some good reason to stand out here on the sidewalk, c'mon inside," he beckoned, and then stared up at the sky. "Clouds beginnin' to scatter. Gonna be a scorcher when they do. Y'all are welcome to have a glass of cold lemonade."

We trailed him up the path to his porch. Patrick nudged me and whispered, "Don't tell my mama, promise?"

"Promise."

The screen door opened and we were ushered inside, where a pretty colored lady wearing a white apron and pink-and-white-checked dress greeted us. "This is my wife, Mrs. Hunter. Phoebe, this is the boy had the bicycle accident yesterday."

Abigail giggled. "The plum fool."

Mrs. Hunter frowned and placed her hand on Abigail's shoulder. "What'd I teach you 'bout saying things that might hurt people's feelings?"

"Not to," she replied.

"And if you go and forget that?"

"I should beg pardon."

Mrs. Hunter rested her hands on her hips and waited.

Somehow Abigail's apology came out sounding like an insult. "Sorry for callin' you a plum fool like my daddy did yesterday."

There was a brief silence followed by Abigail informing me, "Well . . . now you're supposed to say you accept my apology."

"I accept."

Mrs. Hunter took two glasses out of the refrigerator and poured the lemonade. "Keeps it colder this way."

"Thank you, ma'am," I said.

"Thank you, auntie," Patrick told her.

I sipped and studied the house. "Nice place you have," I commented.

"Oh, we're just rentin' here. But it's my dream to have a house of our own someday," Mr. Hunter replied.

Abigail turned to me. "I'm not trying to be rude, but can I ask you a question?" she blurted.

"Ask."

"Why'd you come over here?"

I'd almost forgotten. I turned to Mr. Hunter. "Are you still lookin' for a job, sir?"

"Yessiree. Been lookin' for a real job ever since I got back—"

His wife interrupted him. "Not now" was all she said.

They held on to each other's eyes for a while before he continued, "I sure am. Right now, I grab a little work here and there, fixin' some of the neighbors' cars and other odd jobs."

"Then you oughtta come work for my daddy."

"And what makes you say that?" he asked.

"Because I owe you . . . for savin' me, 'least that's what I was told."

Meriwether shook his head. "You don't owe me nuthin', son."

"Sure I do. Plus, one of his mechanics quit Saturday . . . just ran off to be near his lady friend, and my daddy's been bellyachin' 'bout it. And, like your sign claims, you're good at fixin' things. You know the place. Everyone does. It's called Jake's."

"Jake's? The gas station? One with the garage and car lot?" he asked.

I nodded. "He'll give you a job. I promise."

His eyes flickered with doubt. "You sure about that, Mr. Gabriel?"

"As sure as can be," I said confidently.

Some of the uncertainty disappeared from Meriwether's face. "I suppose it's a fine way to repay a small favor. Thank you, Gabriel."

"You're welcome, but you're wrong about one thing."

"What's that?"

"Fixin' a bicycle is a small favor, but savin' a life is the biggest favor of all," I informed him.

"Those are mighty wise words for someone your age," he commented.

"Twelve. I turned twelve yesterday."

"Twelve—in some places that's practically a man."

Practically a man? I stood up straighter, puffed out my chest, and beamed.

"And the bicycle was your present?" he asked.

"Yessir."

"Well then. Isn't that something." Meriwether patted my shoulder in that fatherly way. "Happy birthday, Gabriel."

"Happy birthday, Gabriel," Mrs. Hunter added.

Abigail finally smiled at me. "Happy birthday for a third time."

"Thank you."

"Folks ever call you Gabe?" Mr. Hunter asked.

"Nossir, not even my mama and daddy . . . Can't say why neither."

Abigail chimed in, "My name means 'a father's delight,' in case you were wonderin'. And most folks never call me Abby neither, but sometimes Mama and my daddy's friends call him Meri and he doesn't mind when they do."

"Sometimes people call me Pat but mostly I don't like it 'cuz it sounds like a girl's name," Patrick said.

To me, right then, the Hunters stopped feeling like new clothes and instead they felt like clothes I'd had awhile—comfortable, like I'd known them a spell.

And by the time we'd finished our lemonade, Mr. Meriwether Hunter had decided to skip his lunch and come with me to Daddy's.

"Can I please go too?" Abigail begged. "I wanna see where you're gonna work."

"Not today," Meriwether replied. "And Phoebe, this might be what we've been waitin' on . . . Say a prayer, you hear?"

"I hear," she replied.

"Thank you for the lemonade, Mrs. Hunter," I told her.

"Yeah, thank you, auntie," added Patrick.

And that was how we left them, Mrs. Hunter standing on the front porch in her pink-and-white dress, Abigail at her side, waving. The man whose wife and friends sometimes called him Meri turned back to them once and waved.

CHAPTER 11

"So, where's your new bicycle today?" Mr. Hunter asked as we walked to my daddy's station.

"Can't ride it for two weeks," I replied.

"Oh, a fortnight is all," he said.

"Huh?" I asked.

"Same as two weeks."

"Did you really call Gabriel a plum fool?" Patrick asked, smirking.

"Well, young one, I'm not prone to lyin' or even stretchin' out the truth. If I recollect, those were my exact words, and now that I think back on it, I should have been more kindly."

"So, all that means you did?" Patrick asked.

He nodded yes. "And it shames me to admit it."

My feelings should have been hurt but they weren't. "I didn't really pay it any mind . . . It's likely what most people been thinkin' anyhow."

Our talk turned to the weather, and then I asked how he'd learned about fixing engines.

As if he were searching for just the right answer, he took a while to reply. "Picked it up here and there. Was told I have something called *mechanical aptitude*."

"Where's here and there?" I continued.

"Round and about," he replied. Right then I realized he was giving me what Mama calls *cloudy answers*. Answers that don't really tell you anything and keep you in the fog.

But that didn't stop me from asking more. "I been wonderin' somethin' 'bout your name."

"What might that be?"

"Did your folks name you after Meriwether Lewis . . . the one who led the Lewis and Clark Expedition?"

"No. 'Twas my daddy's name and belonged to my granddaddy too, likely given to him by the slave master."

"Your granddaddy was a slave?" I asked.

"Yes, and my daddy was a sharecropper . . . someone

who rented land from the man who owned it, and grew and harvested crops. Then they shared the crops."

"Oh, I understand," Patrick spouted. "Share . . . croppers."

"You been livin' in Birdsong long?" I asked.

"Since right before Christmastime. Was born and raised in Charleston. My wife took a job at the Baptist church here, secretary to the pastor, and director of the choir. It's her callin' in life."

"Abigail your only child?"

"So far."

Mr. Hunter shot me a look that told me he was getting tired of questions. And Patrick must have seen it too, because he said, "Don't mind Gabriel askin' all them questions, uncle. He's just been listenin' to too many detective shows on the radio."

That made Mr. Meriwether Hunter laugh.

When we got to Daddy's, Mama was outside. Her car door was open, and she was getting ready to climb in when she saw us.

Quickly, I began the introductions. "Mr. Meriwether Hunter, this is my mama, Agatha, and Mama, this is Mr. Meriwether Hunter, the man from yesterday who pushed me out of the car's way."

"The man who saved a plum fool's life is more like it," Patrick told her.

According to Daddy, Mama is as soft as a ball of cotton with tenderhearted ways, and her tears, whether a reaction to sadness or joy, come easily. That day was the same. Instantly, water dripped from her eyes, and her arms embraced Mr. Meriwether Hunter. "Thank you! Thank you! Thank you!" she said between sobs.

I knew from experience that her clasped arms were strong enough to force almost every iota of air out of a person's lungs. Mr. Hunter squirmed, but Mama only squeezed him tighter. "An angel sent from above!" she squealed. And that was how they were when Daddy showed up. His face spelled confusion.

Seeing Daddy made Mr. Meriwether squirm even more, but he was still firmly in her grip when Daddy said, "Agatha?"

Finally, she released Mr. Hunter and turned her attention to Daddy. "Jake, it's him. The man who saved our Gabriel's life. Thank him and shake his hand!"

Daddy stuck out his hand and Mr. Hunter found it. "Mighty good thing you did for my boy, riskin' your life for his. Thank you kindly, Mr. . . . Meriwether. Is that right?"

"Hunter, Meriwether Hunter," he replied.

"Thank you kindly, Mr. Hunter."

"Right thing to do was all. I have a girl of my own. Our young'uns are mighty precious to us all."

Mama started up again, her enthusiastic words of gratitude bringing the attention of everyone within earshot, including Lucas, Daddy's station attendant and automobile mechanic. "What in tarnation is goin' on out here?" he yelled.

Lucas Shaw was skinny with bowed legs and had hair that was usually in need of a shampoo and a brushing, and Mama and most of the women in town accused him of not having any couth, which was the same as saying he didn't have any manners. As if he was determined to maintain his reputation, he always chewed with his mouth open, spit tobacco, and up close reeked like someone badly in need of a bath.

There was a rumor that he tried three times to enlist after Pearl Harbor got bombed but for some reason was turned away. And the previous year his wife had up and run off, so now he lived with his older sister, who's a dressmaker, and together, they resided in a two-story Victorian house, which was left to them by their mama and daddy. However, couth or no couth, there were two things everyone agreed on: Lucas Shaw was an expert mechanic—but he was also as mean as a raccoon with rabies and for that reason, I didn't like him much.

"This is the fella who saved Gabriel from the accident," Daddy informed him.

"Yeah, from what I heard, it woulda been bye-bye time for you, Gabriel. That Roadmaster woulda mowed you down same as a speedin' train." He cracked a snide grin, showing crooked, tobacco-stained brown teeth.

Mama placed both hands on my shoulders protectively and cried out, "Lucas Shaw, don't you have a speck of kindness in you?"

"Sorry, Mrs. Haberlin. Been told I need a muzzle."

"Nice of you to admit it," Mama replied.

I barged in. "Well, can he have the job, Daddy? He knows all about fixin' cars."

"All about fixin' cars, who?" Lucas asked.

I looked toward Mr. Hunter. "Him."

Lucas cut his eyes at Meriwether and sneered at him while fidgeting with the wrench he was holding. Then he spit a spoonful of tobacco juice right on Meriwether's shoes.

I knew that there were people in Birdsong who were against colored people just because they're colored, but I was shocked to witness this, just the same.

"More than your hands are filthy, Lucas Shaw," Mama lectured him.

Meriwether stared at his shoes, then glared at Lucas.

"Ain't nobody taught you not to stare no white man in the eyes, boy?" Lucas asked.

"That's enough, Lucas," Daddy warned.

Meriwether's hands were at his sides, but I saw him ball the right one into a fist.

Lucas displayed the wrench for all to see.

Mama's face was dressed in worry, and I started wishing I'd never brought Meriwether here.

"Y'all 'bout to fight?" Patrick asked.

Right then a customer drove into the gas station and stopped at the pump. Daddy tapped Lucas on the shoulder and told him to get back to work. Lucas hesitated. "Now!" Daddy ordered, letting him know who was the boss.

Lucas spit once more, but this time nowhere near Meriwether, and headed back to work.

Embarrassment crawled into Mama's eyes. She looked at Meriwether and said, "That man's mouth and mind are fulla ignorance."

"That what you call him?" Mr. Hunter asked. "A man?"

I faced my daddy. "Can he have the job?"

"Sorry," Daddy said. "I'm thinking maybe that's not the best idea now . . ."

I'd always been proud to be Jake Haberlin's son, but right then my feelings began boxing with each other. "Why not? Just 'cuz he's colored? You're always claimin' it isn't fair the way the colored people get treated. Besides, he saved my life. That's worth somethin', isn't it?"

"I could work on the cars and clean up 'round here after hours, sir, do anything that needs doin' . . . Have a wife and a girl at home . . . Been outta regular work for a long spell. Tryin' my best to stay off relief and get back on my feet," Meriwether said.

Daddy hesitated, the way he tends to when he's trying to make certain he's making the right decision, then finally replied, "Seems my son is my conscience." He told Meriwether, "I suppose long as you and Lucas don't cross paths, it might work itself out." Mama squeezed his hand.

It took only a few more moments for him to decide that Meriwether should start the following afternoon. "No need to worry about pumpin' gas. Got a high school boy who comes in after school for that. Name's Matthew. Nice young fella. He closes up 'round nine."

Meriwether grinned. "You won't be sorry, Mr. Haberlin."

Daddy shook Meriwether's hand and said, "Call me Jake. Just promise me one thing."

"What's that?"

"Should you and Lucas happen to cross paths and he becomes . . ." He searched for a word and found it. "Hostile . . . promise me you'll just walk away. Can't know if it's true or not, but there's a rumor he's got friends in a certain organization."

"The KKK?" Meriwether asked, but it was more an answer than a question.

Patrick finally chimed in, "The KKK? They wear white hoods so cain't nobody see their faces. I saw 'em once when I was nine and we were drivin' over 'round Batesburg. There were 'bout ten of 'em ridin' horses and my mama got scared 'cuz she claims they hate Catholics. Never seen KKK in Birdsong, though. Still, Mama warns us to always keep our medals hidden under our shirts." Patrick pulled out his medal, presented it briefly, then tucked it away.

As if to offer comfort, Mama patted Patrick's shoulder.

"So," Meriwether told Patrick, "we're alike . . . you and I."

Patrick scrunched up his face and said, "But you're colored and I'm white, uncle, so we can't be."

I had to laugh. Patrick is one of those people who

sometimes needs to have things spelled out for them, and that's what I did. "He means that the Klan doesn't like coloreds or Catholics, and that means y'all have somethin' in common."

Patrick took a few seconds to understand what he'd just been told. Slowly, a smile appeared. "Oh."

Then the attention returned to Meriwether, and Daddy said, "I'd hate to have you or your family harmed."

"Yes," Mama said. "Long as you stay out of each other's way, Mr. Hunter, I'm sure there won't be any problems, right, Jake?"

Before Daddy could answer, I asked, "How come people do stuff like Lucas just did?"

Meriwether answered for him, "Blindness."

"But Lucas ain't blind. He can see good as all of us," Patrick said.

"All kinda ways to be blind," he said softly, "all kinda ways."

I was about to ask him what he meant, but as soon as I opened my mouth, Lucas slithered by, causing Mama to put her finger to her lips, and I knew my tongue had to be still. And for a while, except for my thoughts, it was quiet.

After Lucas retreated to the garage and the sounds that followed told us he was back to work, Meriwether offered more thanks and headed home. Daddy rushed off, eager to make a deal with a man who was examining the ten or so automobiles on the lot, and Patrick and I climbed into Mama's car.

"*Terror by Night* is playing. Would y'all like to go to a matinee with me?"

"Sherlock Holmes? Hot diggity yes!" I replied.

"You kiddin'? I've been waitin' all week to see it," Patrick said, "but I need to ask my mama."

Mama made a left turn, and in no time at all we pulled up to the curb in front of Patrick's house.

Patrick sprinted inside and soon his mama, Teresa Kelly, appeared on the porch, her stomach big with a child she was expecting any time now, waving a dishrag, grinning, and in a flash Patrick returned and slid into the back seat. Music from the radio filled up the car as we drove, and Mama sang along with Perry Como.

As we coasted along Main Street, I thought about Lucas spitting on Meriwether and whether he really had friends in the KKK, and wondered what other ugly things might be lurking near the pretty town of Birdsong, USA.

CHAPTER 12

There are some things that should never happen when you're twelve and you're standing in the movie line—alongside your mama—but like it or not, they happen just the same. I heard her voice behind me and swiveled around.

"Hi, Mrs. Haberlin and Gabriel," Rosie Riley said. Patrick poked his head out from behind me. "Oh, and Patrick."

Beside her stood her best friend, Emma Kane, who suffers from what Patrick and I call the Triple S disease—snooty, self-worshipping, and selfish.

"Well, hi there, Rosie and Emma," Mama said in her cheerful way.

Patrick offered them a half wave.

Rosie and Emma were there by themselves, and me being with Mama made me feel like I was still a baby. Right then, I wanted to go poof and disappear. "Hi, R-Rosie," I stammered, "and Emma."

"Hiya," Emma said.

"You seem all better from yesterday," Rosie commented.

My face got warm, and I could feel it turn red. "I am, thanks."

The line began to move, and Mama declared, "Thank the Lord. This heat has got it in its mind to do me harm."

"It's true, Mrs. Haberlin, people can die from being too hot. It's called hyperthermia," Rosie said seriously.

Mama winked at her. "I see your daddy's profession is rubbin' off on you."

"Yes ma'am, it is," Rosie replied confidently. Her hair was swept up and held in place by a tortoiseshell comb like the one I bought for my mama Christmas before last. I tried with all my might to stop admiring Rosie, but I was unsuccessful until Emma blew a huge bubble, distracting me.

Finally, we were at the ticket counter. "One adult and two children," Mama told the man in the booth.

I heard Emma giggle. "Bye-bye, little boys," she said sarcastically.

"So long," Rosie said.

"See ya," I replied.

Please don't let them sit near us, I hoped. Thankfully, they didn't. After a while Porky Pig and Daffy Duck had my attention, and by the time Basil Rathbone appeared on the screen, Rosie Riley had slipped out of my mind— well, mostly.

CHAPTER 13

The conversation at dinner that night reminded me of a grasshopper, hopping around from the car Daddy had sold, to Sherlock Holmes, to Rosie being a very smart girl, until it finally landed on Meriwether Hunter.

"Still not sure if this is a good idea . . . Lucas bein' the way he is," Daddy remarked.

Even Mama, who generally tries to see the good side of things, expressed doubts. "It's been gnawin' at me too, Jake."

I had the perfect solution to the problem. "Just fire Lucas. You said before how you'd like to."

"That was before the other fella up and quit. Wasn't

expectin' that. And what if this Meriwether isn't all you think he is? That'd put me in quicksand."

Mama nodded in agreement. "Still, I'd hate to feel responsible for any nasty goings-on."

"Should be some law that keeps you from doin' harm when all you were aimin' to do is good." Daddy sighed.

"Oughtta be but there isn't," Mama commented.

"After y'all left, I tried to settle things down with Lucas. I told him I was hiring Meriwether. That he'd be coming in late, after Lucas was off for the day, and that I'd appreciate it if he could keep the way he feels about coloreds to himself while he's at work . . . should they happen to cross paths."

"What'd he say?" I asked.

"Just said, 'You the boss, Jake.' Then got a sly look on his face and started whistling."

"You really think he's in with the Klan?" I asked.

"Hard to know who is and who isn't," Daddy replied.

"I don't quite understand it," I said. "Lots of the stuff they do is against the law, right?"

"Yes," Daddy answered.

My next question was, "So how come they don't get arrested or put in jail?"

"It's not right, Gabriel," Mama said. "But the South

has its ways. Your daddy and I aren't the only ones in Birdsong who would like things to change, and we're hopin' that one day they will. But I don't want to see you frettin' . . ."

"Not frettin', just wonderin'," I told her.

She rubbed my head. "Gonna wear your young brain out with all that wonderin'. Some things have no answers."

"Maybe there are answers but we just haven't found 'em yet," I replied.

"That could surely be," Daddy said. And then he tried to lighten the mood when he turned to Mama and grinned. "Well, Agatha, how do you like that? We've gone and created us a thinker."

That night, in bed, I thought about whether too much thinking could actually be bad for you. I'd heard people talk about folks who'd worked themselves to death, and I wondered if it was possible for a person to think themselves to death. Right then, I figured that's what sleep is for—to give your mind and body a rest.

I nodded off and dreamed.

CHAPTER 14

The following days were both extra normal and extremely usual. I did my chores, including helping Mama pull weeds from her garden, went swimming with Patrick and his younger brother Joe, tried to catch some fish but didn't have any luck. And because you always miss stuff the first time, I usually try to see a movie twice, so on Thursday, I was going to see the Sherlock Holmes movie again. But because an uncomfortable feeling kept dogging me all week—a feeling I wasn't used to, that something bad was going to happen—I decided that before the movie I'd stop by Daddy's to see how things were working out for Meriwether.

Lucas was just coming out of the bathroom with the sign on the door that said Whites, drying his hands off on a rag. According to the clock, it was twenty minutes past his quitting time and Meriwether was due any minute.

Seemed to me Lucas was making a show of wiping his hands. "Gotta make sure I get all the black off," he said with emphasis on the word *black*. He tossed the rag into the bin and held up his hands for me to see. "Now, that's exactly how I like 'em, Gabriel—nice and white."

I may only be twelve, but I understood what he was getting at, and I hoped he'd be gone before Meriwether showed up. But I hoped wrong, because right then, Meriwether strolled in.

Meriwether greeted us pleasantly. "Good afternoon."

"Hi, Mr. Hunter," I replied.

Lucas responded with a scowl. His usual wad of tobacco was tucked inside his cheek, and I wondered if he was going to spit at Meriwether's feet again, but luckily, he didn't.

Without a word, he walked out into the sun and didn't look back. I stood in the doorway and watched Lucas until he was out of sight. Something was still eating at me inside and had me worried.

"How do you like workin' here?" I asked Meriwether.

He slipped into his coveralls and said, "I like it just fine."

"I would stay but the movie starts at four, and if I do, I'll be late," I explained.

He popped the hood on a car and stuck his head inside. "Wouldn't want that, now, would we?"

"No. I always try to see a movie twice because that way I remember it better."

"Even if you don't like the movie?" he asked.

"The only ones I can't stand are those lovey-dovey sappy ones. And I try never to see those even once."

"Smart boy."

"See ya," I told him.

He raised his head and waved. "Bye now, Gabriel."

And as I walked off, a part of me wanted to skip the movie and go back and talk some more with Meriwether Hunter. But Patrick was waiting on me, so I headed into town.

After dinner, I went to my room and stared at the bicycle I'd been forbidden to ride. Patrick was right. They may as well just crucify me, I thought.

I was still pitying myself when Meriwether dropped

into my mind and lingered there. Some folks were always itching to start trouble, and Lucas was one of them. A kind man had saved my life and that man happened to be colored, and I didn't want anything bad to happen to him.

Inside of me, questions and worries collided with each other, producing more and more, until I had too many. Finally, everything going on inside my skull quieted down and I had my answer.

I'd go to work at the shop. That way, not only could I spend time with Meriwether, who, even though I'd only known him for a short while, for some reason had already started to feel like my friend, but also, with the boss's son nearby, Lucas wouldn't likely start any mess—would he?

CHAPTER 15

Same as most mornings, the newspaper was shielding my father's face when I walked into the kitchen. Bacon frying in the skillet made my mouth water, and I knew hot grits were in the pot next to it. I lifted the lid and inhaled. I was still wearing my nightclothes. It was six thirty.

Mama smiled. "You're up early for a summer mornin'."

"Mornin', son," Daddy said without showing his face.

"Mornin'."

"You want some eggs?" Mama asked.

"Yes ma'am. Sunny side up, please."

"The answer is no," Daddy said. "The bicycle is off-limits for the full two weeks, Gabriel. I'm not gonna budge on this one, and neither is your mama, right, Agatha?"

Mama nodded her agreement.

"I wasn't even gonna ask about the bicycle."

Daddy's face appeared from behind the paper, and he glanced at his watch. "Then what's the matter? Why're you up so early?"

"Nuthin' . . . I was just thinkin'."

"You go to bed thinkin' and wake up thinkin' too? Do you sleep at all?"

"Yessir, like a log," I replied.

He gazed at me in a strange way, as if somehow I'd changed now that I'd turned twelve.

"Your mind still set on becomin' a pilot?" Daddy asked. "Because I'm of the opinion that you might wanna set your sights on a career that pays you to think. Study something like philosophy and become a college professor, maybe a lawyer."

"Nossir. I think a pilot is what I aim to be, or maybe a detective."

"That so." His face disappeared behind the paper again.

"I got up early to tell you I'd like to work at the shop, maybe help Matthew pump gas, wash windows, check the oil, and all that, if you like. It'd be good experience. I'm old enough now. And you don't even have to pay me."

"Free labor. I won't say no to that." He hesitated, and seconds passed. "Plus, you can look after Meriwether that way."

I was a squeaky-clean window—very easy to see through. "Yessir . . . that too."

Mama spoke up. "I do not want my son around that Lucas Shaw." Then she said something I'd never heard her say about anyone before. "He's trash. Wish you could let him go, Jake."

"Can't do that yet, Agatha. Gotta first see if Meriwether works out. So far, he seems to know his way around an engine just fine. But still, I need two mechanics."

Mama set a plate in front of me. "I hope it'll work itself out."

"Gabriel, I'm gonna tell you the same thing I told Meriwether. Lucas starts up with you, don't feed his fire by biting back. I've never had to bring physical harm to another human being and I'd just as well leave it that way, but—"

I looked in his eyes. "But?"

Mama turned away from the sink and faced us. "That's enough, Jake."

"So, it's all right with you?" I asked.

"It's okay. You might even pick up some understanding of automobiles and engines, and there's a clear advantage to learnin' almost any technical skill. I'll even pay you a wage. You can save it for the expensive college I have a feelin' you'll be headin' off to."

Daddy stood up from the table and kissed Mama goodbye.

"What time should I be at work?" I asked.

"Three thirty . . . on the dot."

"On the dot," I repeated.

My parents had said I couldn't ride my bicycle, but they hadn't forbidden me to sit on it. And that's where I was when Patrick showed up, his swimming goggles around his neck. "What you gonna do today?" he asked.

"Got some chores, then I'm goin' to work."

"To work? When'd you get a job?"

"This mornin' . . . Gonna help out at my daddy's."

"He gonna pay you? 'Cuz if he is, tell him I want a job too."

"He's payin' but I think for now he has all the help he needs."

"Yeah, Lucas and Matthew and the uncle and now you, spoze that's enough."

"He's got a name," I barked, "plus, he's not your uncle."

"You talkin' 'bout that colored man?"

"Yes. His name is Mr. Hunter, or Meriwether, if you like . . . but he's not your uncle, so you shouldn't call him that."

Patrick defended himself. "You don't havta get all mad, Gabriel. Colored men are uncles and colored ladies are aunties. That's what a lot of the white folks around here call 'em."

"I don't."

Patrick shrugged.

We were interrupted by Mama. "I'm goin' to get my hair done!" she hollered. "And then stop at the grocery! See y'all later!"

"Bye."

The screen door banged shut and she was gone.

Patrick studied my face and I studied his. "You still mad?" he asked.

This time I shrugged.

THERE ARE THINGS you shouldn't even think about doing when you've gotten off easy—but you do it anyway.

"I'm gonna take it outside and ride it," I informed Patrick.

"But?"

"It's the same as puttin' food in front of a hungry man and tellin' him not to eat. Sooner or later when no one's lookin', he's bound to take a bite, isn't he?"

"If it was me, I sure would. Pro'bly eat it all up," Patrick agreed.

"I just gotta."

"What if you get caught?"

"It's the worst temptation ever. Almost like they're daring me, makin' me look at it day and night. The way I figure, it's not my fault for givin' in, it's theirs for temptin' me."

Patrick thought for a while and responded, "Yeah . . . they're to blame, that's for sure. Can I ride it too?"

"Yeah, but if you breathe a word to anyone, I'll never let you ride it again. Promise?"

"Cain't promise," he replied.

"How come?"

"If someone asks and I lie, then I gotta tell it in confession."

"Okay, but not your mama or anyone else. Cross your heart and hope to die?"

"Cross my heart and hope to die," he replied.

Fearing someone might see us and squeal, I only circled the block once and then let Patrick do the same. And then we parked it back in my room.

"Think that'll do you until the two weeks are up?" Patrick asked.

"Can't say for sure . . . Maybe, maybe not."

"Well, if you decide you're gonna ride it some more, wait for me so I can ride it too, word of honor?"

"Word of honor."

CHAPTER 16

I'd never had a job before, but from what I've heard folks say, there are things a person should do if they plan to keep it—things like being on time, doing your work without complaining, and never stealing anything, even if it's worth less than a penny.

Daddy checked his watch when I stepped through the door. "Thank you for being prompt, Gabriel."

"Is Lucas here?" I asked.

"Three o'clock is quittin' time for him. Unless he's in the middle of something important, soon as that second hand hits the twelve, he's in the wind."

The clock on the wall read three fifteen.

My next question was, "Is Meriwether here?"

"Should be here soon. Usually sticks his head in when he gets here so we can talk about what needs to get done. But c'mon now. Time for you to learn to work the pumps," Daddy said, "and remember, even if you don't feel like it, always greet your customer with a smile."

As luck would have it, my very first customer of the day was the one who had almost taken my life, Mrs. Betty Babcock. It wasn't Sunday, but as always, Betty Babcock was, as Mama says, all done up. Her lips were painted bright orange, a gold necklace and earrings sparkled in the sunlight, and a long pink scarf was tied around her neck.

As soon as she saw me, Mrs. Betty Babcock hopped out of her car. "Hello, y'all!" she hollered.

As instructed, I smiled. "Hi, Mrs. Babcock. You want me to fill it up?"

"You ain't but just turned twelve and your daddy has got you workin'. Shouldn't you be off enjoyin' the summer like other people your age?"

"I wanna work, ma'am. It's my first day."

"Suppose you'll be takin' over this business from your daddy someday?"

I'd actually never thought about that, but the sound of what she'd said felt to me like a piece for the wrong puzzle, something that was never going to fit. "Don't think so, ma'am," I replied.

She winked at Daddy. "Hope you're at least payin' the boy, Jake."

"He is," I told her. I was raring to get to it. "Should I fill it up?"

"Twenty-one cents a gallon? Strange how I never noticed the price of gasoline until I started drivin'. It's pure thievery, Jake. Can't you do something about these prices?" she asked, then winked again.

"Out of my hands, Betty."

She turned to me. "I reckon you need the experience . . . so may as well fill it. And check the oil too, and while you're at it, Gabriel, my windows could use a good cleanin'."

I knew how to fill a tank and washing windows was a cinch, but I'd never checked oil. I gave my daddy the I-need-help look.

"Gabriel, hold off on fillin' the tank and let me show you how to check the oil." He popped the hood and yanked a rag from his pocket. As he worked, he schooled me step by step until he was done. "Then you put the dipstick back where it came from and close the hood." He closed the hood. "Oil's fine, Betty."

"Wait a minute," I said. "Where does the oil go if I havta put some in?"

"Tomorrow's lesson."

"Tomorrow's Saturday and we're going to Charleston for the parade," I reminded him.

"Next week, then. For now, anyone comes in needin' anything more than gas and clean windows, have Matthew see to it. And if it's something major and I'm not around, Meriwether's inside the garage."

"Even air in the tires?" I asked.

He frowned. "Especially air in the tires. Your first week or so is gonna be mostly learnin'. Got one word of advice: if you find yourself in doubt . . . don't do anything. Understand?"

"I do."

By the time Betty Babcock climbed back into the Buick, her tank was full and her windows were as clean as I could get them. She screeched away, the scarf around her neck waving in the wind.

As soon as she sped off, another customer rolled in. "This car drinks up gasoline faster than a thirsty man drinks water," the man said. I smiled and agreed.

"Fill 'er up?" I asked.

"Five gallons oughtta do."

Minutes later, Matthew, who's mostly called Matt, arrived and took over, allowing Daddy to retreat to his office to "shuffle papers." And when a car drove up that needed oil, Matt sent me to the garage to get some. Resting against the wall outside was an old bicycle I'd never seen before, and inside, Meriwether had arrived and was working. "Hi, Mr. Hunter."

He peered out from underneath the hood. The sweat on his dark brown forehead made it glisten, and he wiped at it with the back of his hand. "Hi there, Gabriel."

"I'm workin' here now," I informed him.

"So I've been told," he replied.

"That your bicycle outside?" I asked.

"Not exactly . . . Friend of mine let me borrow it. Beats walkin'."

My eyes searched the shelves for the oil until they found it. "But you have a car. There were two in the driveway at your house."

"Not mine—fixin' 'em for folks is all."

"You'll have a car someday, Mr. Hunter. I betcha."

"If you're worryin' yourself because I don't have a car . . . there's no need," he said, smiling. "I can see you suffer from the same affliction as lots of folks, Gabriel."

"What's that?"

"Only bein' able to see things through the two eyes on your face instead of four or sometimes even more."

"But all I have is two . . . same as you." I wanted to keep talking, but Matt was waiting on the oil. "Be right back after I take him this oil," I told Meriwether.

In a jiffy, I rejoined him in the garage and asked, "About seein' things with more than two eyes, is it some kind of riddle?"

Meriwether leaned his back against the car. "Not a riddle, just one of those things called a great truth. Let me help you understand it." He paused and looked upward, gathering the thoughts he was about to put into words.

I waited patiently.

"Whenever possible, you gotta try to see the goings-on of life through more eyes than just your own, because that can help you see things more clearly. Sometimes it'll even let you see things the way they really are and give you peace of mind. You understand?"

I didn't, so I shrugged.

"It's like this. The way you see it has you hopin' that I'll have a car someday, right?"

I nodded.

"On the other hand, the way I see it allows me to be content because I'm just one of many in South

Carolina—in the whole of these United States, for that matter—who don't have an automobile, and for now that bicycle gets me where I need to go. But when I look at it through four eyes—my two plus your two—I can be both content and have hope. That's why four eyes are usually better than two. And the more eyes you look through, the better you see things—understand now?"

"Kinda. Like if there are ten people with cameras and they're standing around at ten different spots and they all click a picture of the same mountain at the same time, all the photographs are bound to be different. And afterward, lookin' at all ten pictures instead of just one is gonna show you what that mountain really looks like."

Meriwether grinned. "Got a good mind, don't you?"

I chuckled. "Mama and Daddy say I think too much."

"A talent for thinkin's a mighty nice thing to have."

"Thinkin's not a talent," I told him.

"Sure it is," Meriwether replied.

Two car honks came from outside, and I realized Matt probably needed my help. "See ya!" I exclaimed, and made a dash.

CHAPTER 17

Matt didn't talk much, but he smiled and whistled a lot, which I took as evidence of his cheerful nature.

I watched as he checked engine oil and tire pressure, trying to organize the steps in my mind.

And that's what I was doing when the colored pastor drove up and told me, "Fill it up, son—drivin' clear to Georgia."

There were only two gas stations in Birdsong. One was on the way into town and the other was on the way out, depending on which way you were headed. But regardless of your direction, my daddy's was the only one that served coloreds. Jake's had a colored bathroom and water fountain, and I'd once heard Daddy claim that Mrs. Masters, who now and then helps Mama at the house, had shown him something called *The Negro Motorist Green Book*, which lists places, including his, where colored people are welcome to eat, or rest, or get gasoline when they're traveling around. That was when I discovered that being colored and being Negro are the exact same thing.

Once his tank was full, the pastor paid, said, "Thank you kindly," and sputtered off, his tailpipe smoking a little.

I glanced at the Colored restroom sign and started to wonder about what Tink had claimed about all those things being gone someday, but my thinking was interrupted by a customer and then another after that. Busyness and thinking seem to work against each other— with busyness usually winning.

Much later, when I saw Meriwether, he was sitting outside beside the bicycle, legs stretched out and crossed in front of him, chomping on a sandwich. A brown paper bag rested beside him. "Suppertime," he commented.

I studied the bicycle again.

"Not much when you compare it with your new

Schwinn, is it? Betcha can't wait to ride it again, huh?"
Meriwether asked.

Before I realized it, I'd opened my mouth. "I already
did," I confessed.

"So, they took you off punishment?"

I shook my head no.

He chuckled. "Oh, you snuck and did it. Was it fun?"
he asked.

I hadn't even thought about that. I hesitated before
I answered. "Mostly, but not the same as the first time I
rode it."

"Guilt can do that," he said. "Take the fun out."

Quietness settled in around us.

And then suddenly, a lot of words spilled out of me.
"They put it in my room and forced me to look at it. All
that did was tempt me . . . until I finally gave in. If they'd
made me keep it in the garage, it might have kept it out of
my mind and maybe I wouldn't have done it. Anyhow, I
figure it's their fault for temptin' me."

Meriwether Hunter reached in his bag, pulled out
an apple, took a huge bite, and chewed. Finally, he swal-
lowed and spoke. "The way I see it, they put it there to
teach you a lesson. That's what punishment's for. You

bein' tempted was how the punishment made you feel. And if you hadn't surrendered, it likely would have made you stronger. Resistin' temptation builds strength. We fail when we give in to it."

"So, I failed?"

"Yes, my young friend, you failed. But what's important now is whether you fail again." He took another bite from his apple.

I stared at him, and was mulling it over when a car honked, forcing me to make a beeline to the pump.

And that evening when I got home, I traced the bicycle's handlebars and counted. Nine days left.

This was going to be hard, but I was determined not to fail again.

CHAPTER 18

A person who hasn't taken this ride as many times as I have might call the sights along the way interesting. But the drive from Birdsong to Charleston during the summertime is usually the same.

While Daddy drove, Mama hummed and sang along with the radio music. Now and then they'd talk to each other or me about this or that, but there really wasn't that much conversation. I imagined that if Patrick had come along like he was supposed to, we'd be busy yakking, but that morning Doc Riley had said his mama was about ready to have the baby, and for that reason Patrick had to stay close. So, for over an hour I mostly daydreamed, but if sometime later a person had asked me about what, I probably wouldn't have been able to tell them. In that way, my daydreams are much the same as the dreams that happen along when I'm asleep, for the most part—forgotten.

I knew we were close to the shore when the salty-air smell hit me, followed by the sounds of seagulls. Soon, the Atlantic Ocean came into view and I gazed out to the horizon where the dark blue of the water and the lighter blue of the sky meet.

"Such a lovely breeze," Mama noted. "A trifle cooler than Birdsong."

Before long, we had turned the corner to Tradd Street, where Cousin Polly and Them live. The American flag flapped from the pole holder on the front porch of their big three-story, cream-colored house. The walkway was lined with blooming rosebushes, mostly red.

I was just out of the car when the screen door of the house next to theirs opened and a girl about Tink's age stepped out. She was dressed in a white shirt and blue dungarees rolled up to her knees. Her long curly hair was a color smack-dab between red and brown. She was one of those people who stand out from the rest, a thing you have no choice but to notice first, a full moon in a sea of small stars on a clear night.

Mama and Daddy glanced her way too. "Must be that friend of Tink's from New York City," Mama said.

I searched through my memories for her name until I found it. "Helene."

Like a cat burglar, Helene quietly stole my attention. And my eyes were forced to remain glued on her as I followed Mama and Daddy up the path to Cousin Polly's. When I suddenly tripped on the uneven walkway and stumbled, I expected her to laugh like Emma probably would have, but Helene only smiled a smile that, maybe because I didn't want to see it or maybe because it really wasn't there, contained no meanness.

"Stop gawking, Gabriel," Mama warned.

Daddy turned to me and winked.

"Seems nice," I remarked.

In a blink, she headed inside, and right after her door closed, the doorway to Cousin Polly's opened. "What's buzzin', cuzzins?" Tink said. Her Kodak camera swung from her neck.

Mama nearly had one foot inside when Teddy, Auntie Rita, and Cousin Polly crowded the doorway.

"Dang it and a half! Y'all 'bouta make us late to see your own brother!" Cousin Polly chastised my daddy, waving a finger, nearly touching his nose. "And Earl's only got one day in Charleston b'fore he's gotta head back to base! Oughtta be ashamed but I can see from the grin on your face that you ain't. 'Least I had the decency to make him a party."

Daddy barked back. "Saw him just last month, Polly. For a while there when he was in the hospital, I went to see him once a week. Plus, you offered to have the party. So you got no right to have a hissy."

Auntie Rita piped up. "You know how she is, Jake . . . could start a fuss in an empty house."

"That's 'bout enough, Mama," Teddy warned.

Polly cut her eyes at Rita and yapped some more. "Parade starts in twenty minutes. Lucky for us it's just a few blocks over. Let's get crackin' so we can get a good spot. Wanna make sure Earl sees our lovely smilin' faces in the crowd."

Auntie Rita cleared her throat and chuckled.

Three colored ladies dressed like maids stood inside and were about to close the door when Cousin Polly stopped in her tracks. "Don't y'all gals eat none of that food, you hear?"

"Yes ma'am, Mrs. Polly," they replied.

The door shut, and together, we strolled along.

"Your friend Helene, is she goin' to the parade?" I asked Tink.

"Helene?"

I glanced at Helene's house as we passed by. "She was outside a minute ago—'least I supposed it was her."

"Long, kinda curly hair?"

I nodded yes.

"And if you had to describe her to someone, you'd say she's likely the prettiest girl you ever saw?"

I nodded again.

"That's her, but nossiree Bob, she's definitely not goin' . . . Claims parades are provincial and she wouldn't dare be seen at one."

"Provincial?"

"Unsophisticated," she explained. "If it weren't for cousin Earl, I'd be keepin' my keister home too. But she's comin' for the party because she's dyin' to have her picture taken with a real live genuine American war hero. I can't wait for you to meet her. She's in the know about so many things . . . You'll go absolutely bonkers over her."

I turned to get another glimpse of Helene's house.

And Tink noticed. "Or maybe you already have."

Tink stared at me until I smiled, and the way a smile sometimes can, mine gave me away. Tink nudged me with her shoulder.

Right then, my eyes landed on my tennis shoes. They

were old, but at least I was wearing my favorite blue button-down shirt.

Some things definitely should make you feel ashamed. For instance, when you're heading to a parade for war heroes, and you're about to see your favorite and only uncle, whom you haven't laid eyes on for a while—but before the parade begins, all you can think about is when it's going to end, so you'll be in the same room with a girl who's way too old for you. One glimpse of Helene had pushed Uncle Earl into the back seat of my mind, and something like that should have given me at least a small dose of shame. But it didn't. And I guessed that was part of being twelve.

Hordes lined both sides of the streets, most waving miniature American flags, and ladies and girls were armed with open parasols and umbrellas. Straw and cowboy hats shielded other heads. It was hours before noon, but today's sun was already a scorching one. A man on stilts was dressed up like Uncle Sam, and kids danced around him while smaller children sat on men's shoulders to get a better look. Clowns with painted faces juggled balls and bowling pins while others did cartwheels and acrobatic flips—a sort-of circus without a big top.

"Plenty of patriots out today," Teddy remarked as he set up the folding chair he'd been lugging.

Auntie Rita plopped right into it and had just opened her umbrella when an orange-and-black butterfly landed on her arm. "What a good omen!" she proclaimed.

"Why?" I asked.

"Legend has it that if a butterfly lands on you and you say a prayer, it flies clear to heaven with it to make sure it gets answered right away," she explained.

"All the way to heaven? That's a mighty long trip, Auntie Rita," I said with a smile.

"A legend's just a myth and myths are mostly just made up, Nana," Tink said. "Nuthin' can fly clear to heaven . . . except maybe angels."

Auntie Rita gazed upward. "I got nuthin' to say but amen."

The parade began with about twenty girls dressed alike in sparkly red, white, and blue, twirling silver batons. The leader signaled them to stop, and simultaneously, they tossed the shining batons high in the sky. Then, they swiveled around and caught them behind their backs. Except the smallest girl, who missed hers and started to cry.

A marching band was right on their heels, playing

"Boogie Woogie Bugle Boy," their polished brass instruments and uniform buttons gleaming. Folks, including Mama, Auntie Rita, and even Tink and Teddy, sang along to the music. Cousin Polly hummed and Daddy tapped his foot. Trumpets make a most agreeable sound, I thought.

The first convertible in the motorcade held two uniformed men, and one of them was my uncle—Lieutenant Earl Haberlin.

Uncle Earl removed his hat and waved to the crowd. Whistles, hoots, yelps, and hollers came from everywhere, hands clapped, and voices cheered loudly, the noise nearly drowning out the band.

I jumped up and down, waving both my hands to get his attention, and when our eyes finally met, my uncle Earl, a true-blue American war hero, stood and saluted.

Tink snapped another picture.

"Can you get an extra print made of that photo you just took?" I asked her. "One for me, so I can always remember?"

My cousin smiled and said, "You betcha!"

CHAPTER 19

While we waited for the party to get started, Tink and I listened to music on the radio upstairs in her bedroom. The windows were wide open and a fan purred. While she danced around, the way she likes to do with her eyes half closed, singing and swirling with the music, I thumbed through her photos.

As I flipped through them, I noticed there were more than a few photos of Helene. In all of them she looked beautiful, but in one she was staring directly into the camera, smiling, with a look in her eyes that I couldn't figure out—something different. And then, as if I had no control over my actions, I slyly slipped that one into my back pocket. Instantly, my mind defended the thievery by reminding me that Tink always keeps her negatives. She could always have a copy made if she missed it and wanted another.

Suddenly, she stopped dancing and I wondered if she'd seen me, but all she said was, "Wanna see my portfolio?"

I sighed. "Sure."

The only thing I know about photographs is that I like looking at some more than others. But as Tink held up one after another for me to see, I found myself wanting to keep staring at all of them for a while.

"Helene's daddy says I have a talent for it . . . You think he's right?"

I nodded my agreement.

Then she held up a picture of a colored girl on a bicycle beside a whites-only drinking fountain. "I think this is one of my best," she claimed.

I studied it for what seemed like a long time. "Did she drink from it?" I asked.

"'Course not."

Silently, I wondered if she'd been thirsty and tempted, and if the feeling the sign gave her had a stink to it or if maybe she was used to the bad smell by now.

"If she had drunk from it and someone had seen her, do you think they'd take a girl to jail?"

"Probably not . . . just get her mama and daddy after her."

"Likely get a loud chastisin' from them?"

"Likely."

Right then, my thoughts flipped to something else. "You think the water tastes any different in the colored fountain?"

Tink looked me square in the face. "It doesn't," she replied.

"How do you know?"

"We drank from the colored fountain . . . just last week. Me and Helene. She did it first. So I did it too."

"Did anyone see you?"

"One old lady."

"White or colored?"

"White."

"Then what?"

"She accused us of being twelve shades of crazy. But Helene just took another sip of water and told her, 'I'm a citizen of the United States of America, which is supposed to mean, white or colored, I am free to drink water from wherever I please.'

"That made the woman start actin' hainty, and she asked Helene where she was from. 'New York City,' Helene told her."

"Then what?" I asked.

"The woman called her a Yankee troublemaker and told her if she didn't like the ways of South Carolina to take a fast train back to New York City. Helene just laughed at her, until finally the woman walked away, all the while cussin' us out."

In my mind, I pictured the beautiful girl from New York City in the photograph I'd just stolen—the girl Cousin Polly called Helen-with-an-E—and knew then what it was I'd seen in her eyes. It was bravery.

CHAPTER 20

Later, Tink and I were sitting on the front porch swing, waiting for Daddy and Teddy to come back with Uncle Earl, when a man wearing a blue bow tie and lugging a large camera strolled up the path. He was a stick-thin brown-haired man with more freckles than I'd ever seen. "I'm the photographer from the *Charleston Evenin' Post*. This the Waldrop place?" he asked.

"Yessir," we answered. Tink got up and touched her camera as she inspected his. From the hungry look in her eyes I immediately sensed that his was something she was itching to have.

He must have recognized the same expression, because

he smiled at Tink and informed her, "It's a Graflex Speed Graphic four-by-five press camera . . . in case you were wonderin'."

"A Graflex Speed Graphic four-by-five press camera," she repeated as if she were storing it in her memory. "Is it an awful lot of fun . . . bein' a real photographer?" she asked.

"Generally, I find it enjoyable. An interested individual oughtta possess immense patience and an adventuresome nature."

"I've got that—the adventuresome nature at least," Tink responded confidently.

He smiled again. "Your folks inside?"

Tink stood, went over to the door, and hollered through the screen, "Photographer's here . . . says he's from the newspaper, Mama!"

"The newspaper? Comin'!"

I'd never seen Polly run, but from the sound of her shoes clicking on the wood floor, I could tell she was doing just that.

He and Cousin Polly chatted, and when he left to go get more equipment from his car, Polly informed us, "He's from the *Charleston Evening Post*. Can y'all believe it? Wants pictures of the house too." She touched her hair and fingered the collar of her polka-dotted blouse. "Suppose I should go make myself decent." Polly's eyes fell on Tink. "You too, Theodora. Go put on a pretty dress."

"No, thank you, Mama, I'm decent enough," she replied.

"Suit yourself . . . Can y'all believe it?" Polly ripped open the screen door and practically danced into the house. "Photographer from THE *Charleston Evening Post* is here, y'all!" she yelled, emphasizing the word *the*.

"She'll be puttin' on airs for the next ten years," Tink confided.

Because I knew it was true, I had to laugh.

SOON, SMILING GUESTS began spilling out of their cars and alongside others who'd traveled on foot they made their way toward Cousin Polly and Them's house. Several entering guests were invited by the bow-tie-wearing photographer to pose. I studied my cousin Tink as she examined his every move.

In what felt like no time at all, the inside of the house was as packed as a can of sardines, causing some folks to pour outside onto the wraparound porch and into the big backyard, where there were two gazebos and blooming flowers galore. Cousin Polly had put on quite a show—not for Earl but for herself and the neighbors, Auntie Rita gossiped.

One of the colored maids moved in and around the crowd, offering little finger foods, including my favorite, deviled eggs. I grabbed two. Just like Mama's, they were sprinkled with paprika. I stuffed one whole into my mouth, and the second was right behind it. Boy, was I hungry for some real food. And for that reason, I headed to the kitchen.

Another maid was pulling a pie out of the oven, and a platter of sliced ham was on the table.

I eyed the ham. "I'm 'bout starvin'," I told her.

She sat the hot pie on the counter, then inspected me. "I seen you 'round here a few times b'fore. You Miss Tink's cousin, ain't ya?" she asked.

"Yes ma'am, Gabriel." I tried to recall her face but couldn't.

"Almost growed up, huh?"

I shrugged. "Spoze. I just turned twelve."

"I could make you a sandwich," she offered. "Think that might could keep ya from starvin' for a spell?"

"Yes ma'am, it surely might. Thank you." I gazed at her. She looked to be as old as Auntie Rita, and her black maid's dress was old too. A net covered her gray hair, and her white apron was soiled from cooking. Something about her finally rang a faint bell inside me—and I remembered a time or two I'd seen her here before.

She poked around inside the refrigerator. "Mayonnaise or mustard?" she asked.

"Both, please."

She motioned at the kitchen table and chairs and ordered, "Sit down, young mister."

I did as I was told. "What's your name, ma'am?" I asked.

"Auntie."

"No, I mean your real name," I told her.

"Johnnie Dove . . . That's two words. Johnnie Dove Victory. But I'm called Dovey by most."

"Pleased to meet ya, Mrs. Victory."

"You mean that or you just sayin' it 'cause I'm fixin' to save ya from starvin'?"

That made me chuckle.

"The man they's havin' this party for, he was a flier, weren't he?" she asked.

I beamed. "My uncle Earl . . . yes ma'am. Shot down more than a few Nazi planes. He's a gen-u-wine American war hero."

"Mighty kind of ev'ryone to celebrate his homecomin'," she commented. Then she abruptly stopped what she was doing and gazed through the window. There was still noise all around but somehow it felt quiet. "My son was in the United States Navy," she revealed. "Served out yonder in the Pacific. Even got hisself a Good Conduct Medal. Last letter he sent said soon as the war got done, he was gonna move to San Francisco and send for me and his daddy. He falled head over hills in love with California . . . Only spent a few days there but claimed it got in his blood."

"Is that where he is now?" I asked.

"No, child. He's gone."

"Where?"

"To heaven, I hope. Got killed out in New Guinea . . . You heard of New Guinea?"

"Yes ma'am. I think it's near Australia."

She nodded in agreement. "That's right. I never even knowed there was sucha place 'til . . ." Her voice trailed off. "Last time he was seen alive, he was helpin' carry wounded American soldiers to safety. Then, accordin' to what his friend wrote us, there was a big explosion and he was gone. Makin' things worse, only thing they found was his dog tags . . . but his body ain't never been located.

"I finally gived up prayin' on that. Woulda been nice,

though, to have a proper burial with a fancy stone grave marker. That way I could go sit there, bring him a few flowers, talk to him kinda like I used to when he was a li'l boy. I'll never forget the evenin' when the telegram came, nearly cried m'self blind. Sometimes durin' my dreams I still hear that knock on the door and the man's voice sayin' 'Western Union.'"

It felt like a cloud of sorrow had floated into the room. "Sorry, ma'am. What was his name?"

"Homer Lee Bartholomew Victory. Lord have mercy, he was handsome in that navy uniform. Pleaded with him day and night not to enlist, but he was deaf to our words." She hesitated for a moment before continuing, "Sure was proud to be in the United States Navy, though." She pressed on her eyes, the way people do when they're trying to keep back tears. "He was our onliest child, a real good boy, my Homer Lee. And Lord, was he smart. Had a college scholarship to Claflin over in Orangeburg, but the war changed all that. Miss him somethin' awful."

"Sorry, ma'am," I repeated.

She sighed deeply. "Forgive me, son, for carryin' on," she said when she placed the sandwich and a glass of lemonade on the table in front of me.

"It's okay, ma'am."

"Wan'a sweet pickle? They's fresh and crisp."

"Yes ma'am."

She studied my face. "You a right nice young fella, ain't ya?"

"Mostly," I told her, and took a huge bite from my sandwich.

"Nice talkin' to you," she said, then chuckled before adding, "Then again, mostly all you done was listen. So, thank you for list'nin' to an old woman go on and on."

"You're welcome, Mrs.—" As usual, I'd forgotten her name.

"Mrs. Victory . . . Johnnie Dove Victory, mostly called Dovey."

"Thank you, Mrs. Victory. And I'm real sorry about your son, Homer."

CHAPTER 21

Every time the front screen door opened, I crossed my fingers, hoping it would be either Uncle Earl or Helene stepping in, but so far, neither had shown up. Tink was still busy tailing the photographer, but now and then she'd shoot a look my way and smile.

I planted myself in a chair, thought about Mrs. Victory, and imagined that all of us being here to celebrate a soldier's safe homecoming was likely doubling her sadness.

Soon Mama headed my way. "You havin' a nice time, Gabriel?"

"Yes ma'am."

But I guess my face must have looked out of sorts, because she asked, "Why so gloomy, then?"

I didn't have time to answer, because at that moment Daddy and Teddy arrived with the guest of honor, my uncle Earl. More than eight medals, some silver and others gold, were pinned to his uniform jacket.

Of course, the cheering commenced again. Except this time, because we were indoors, it seemed fifty times as loud.

Uncle Earl's a little taller than Daddy, with the same light brown hair, and according to most people, he looks something like Clark Gable without the mustache. I sprang up and wriggled through the swarm that had instantly surrounded him, and tapped his shoulder. "Hi, Uncle Earl," I said.

He turned, bear-hugged me, and lifted me off the ground. "Gabriel!"

The photographer pointed his camera and nearly blinded us with the flash.

Standing beside him, with his arm resting on my shoulder, I proudly listened along with the rest of his admirers to his war stories. Earl Haberlin was just about as entertaining as any radio show as he told us the number of Nazi planes he and his squadron had shot down.

He spun riveting tales of the Battle of the Bulge and how cold and snowy it was, and how it was actually called the Ardennes Counteroffensive until the newspapers changed the name. "I guess Battle of the Bulge had a better ring to it," he said.

Then he captivated us when he gave us a blow-by-blow description of his near demise, as he called it. "I figured I was definitely a goner when my plane took some bullets and started smokin', but somehow I was fortunate enough to make it back to British soil before I had to crash-land."

"Were you scared?" someone asked.

Earl's eyes darted around at his audience. "Spoze y'all would expect me to say no, but that'd be a lie. Can tell you this, though: if my life had ended that day, 'least I woulda died doin' what I could to make this world better instead of worse."

A woman wearing a blue feathered hat who was frantically fanning herself hollered, "Ain't that the gospel truth!"

Many heads nodded in agreement, and Auntie Rita shouted, "Amen!"

And that was when the screen door swung open for probably the hundredth time. This time Helene stepped inside.

Helene quickly zeroed in on Tink and the newspaper photographer and squirmed her way through the crowd to reach them. Before I knew it, Helene was posed beside Uncle Earl, several pictures had been taken, and in no time flat, Helene and Tink were standing beside me near the door. To draw attention to myself, I cleared my throat loudly.

Tink got the idea right away and introduced us. "Helene, this is my cousin Gabriel. Gabriel, this is Helene."

"Hi" was all I could manage to say.

"Nice to meet you, Gabriel," Helene said. "But I have to go. Toodle-oo."

"Toodle-oo," Tink replied.

Understanding it meant *goodbye* but wishing it didn't, I told her, "Toodle-oo."

In no time at all, Tink had scurried back to the photographer's side.

But I stayed nestled in the doorway, watching Helene as she strode confidently toward her house, hoping all the while she'd turn around just once and glance my way, but she didn't. "Toodle-oo," I whispered.

CHAPTER 22

If Sunday had been mostly normal and dull without any extra shine to it, Monday sure wasn't. Meriwether arrived at work on foot, frowning, and Abigail was with him.

"Where's the bicycle?" I inquired.

Abigail answered, "Someone stole it."

"Right from here," Meriwether added. "I came in on Saturday like your daddy asked me to 'cause cars needin' to be fixed were backed up. And when I went to leave that evenin', it was nowhere to be found. Strange I didn't hear anything, but then again, I had the radio goin'. Matthew didn't see nuthin' either."

Before I could stop myself, I'd said it. "Lucas."

"That's exactly what my daddy thought," Abigail confided.

"Likely it's true but I got no proof. Now I gotta pay to replace my buddy's bicycle." He sighed loudly. "And my wife had some family business to tend to in Savannah, so Abigail has to be here with me a few days. Hope that's all right with your daddy. He in his office?"

"Was last time I saw him."

Meriwether pointed to a chair and said to his daughter, "Sit there and don't say anything that's certain to rob me of any pride I might have in you, understand?"

"Is that the same as tellin' me to be good?" she asked.

"The exact same. Read your book like you promised. Can you do that?"

As instructed, Abigail plopped down, opened a book in her lap, and responded, "Yessir, I can."

I was on Meriwether's heels. "You gonna tell my daddy 'bout Lucas?"

"Gonna give him the facts. Only thing I got proof of is the bicycle's missin'. Can't say who."

"No clues or witnesses," I asked.

"Not a one."

"But a definite suspicion as to who might have committed the crime?" I added.

Meriwether chuckled. "Your friend Patrick's right: you have been listenin' to too many late-night detective shows."

Before Meriwether had a chance to open his mouth, I blurted, "I know it was Lucas, Daddy."

Daddy put down his pencil and looked up from his ledger. "Lucas?"

"Who stole Mr. Hunter's bicycle."

"Is that true?" he asked Meriwether.

"It's true that the bicycle disappeared Saturday evenin' from the side of the garage where I generally leave it. As far as who dunnit, that I can't say. Didn't see anyone or hear anything."

"Can't accuse a man without proof," Daddy said.

"Nossir, can't, but I got favors to ask. My wife is away for a few days and I'm wonderin' if it'd be all right if my girl, Abigail, stays in the garage with me while I work. She won't be any trouble. Just gonna sit and read."

"All right by me . . . And?" Daddy asked. "You said favors—that's plural."

"That black '36 Chevy 'round back. If it's for sale, I'm

hopin' I might buy it on one of those installment plans I hear you offerin' folks. You could hold the money outta my pay if need be."

"That heapa junk? Can't no one even get it to start, and some of the best have tried. I tell you what, Meriwether, you get that thing runnin', it's yours paid in full. Was 'bout to sell it for scrap."

"You jokin' with me, Jake?"

Daddy cracked a grin. "The joke might be on you with that car."

Meriwether, now smiling, stretched out his hand. "It's a deal, then?"

They shook and Daddy replied, "Deal."

But before we could leave, Daddy put on a grim face. "Be best if y'all keep your suspicions 'bout Lucas and the bicycle to yourselves . . . seein' as we got no proof."

"Learned a long time ago when to keep my mouth shut," Meriwether told him.

"That includes you, Gabriel. Not even a word to Patrick . . . clear?"

"Yessir, clear."

Instantly, my daddy's face switched back to pleasant.

"About that car, what if you can't fix it? . . . No one else has been able to," I remarked as Meriwether and I headed toward the garage.

"You're forgettin' two things, young man."

"What?"

"Number one, I'm not *no one else*. And number two, I *am* Meriwether Hunter. And I'm mighty good at fixin' things."

Abigail was right where we'd left her, reading. She glanced up. "Did he say I could stay?"

Meriwether nodded. "But you gotta do like you promised, Abigail."

"I am," she said, holding up the book. "B'sides, no one has to make me read. I'm already on page fifteen."

"Whatcha readin'?" I asked.

"*The Magical Land of Noom.* It's from the library at church."

"Churches don't have libraries," I informed her.

"Ours does. Pastor and my mama started one 'cause there're hardly any books like this . . . you know . . . for children"—she waved the book at me—"in the colored section in the Birdsong library . . . maybe only five, and I've read 'em all."

Meriwether chimed in, "They were gonna have the

library at the school, but havin' it at the church lets almost anyone check out a book if they like." He popped the hood of a car and got to work.

"But only one book at a time," Abigail said. Then she asked, "Have you read *The Boxcar Children*?"

"No."

"What about *The Cat Who Went to Heaven*?"

I shook my head.

"Whatsamatter with you . . . Can't you even read?"

"What kinda question is that? 'Course I can."

Meriwether looked up from the car engine. "Abigail?"

"Sir?"

"Watch yourself. And Gabriel . . . don't mind her. She likes to brag on herself about all her readin'."

"Right before school ended, I read *The Yearling*," I boasted.

"Parts of it were too sad . . . made me cry," Abigail declared.

Because it was the only book that had ever brought me to tears, I was about to agree, but before I could say anything, embarrassment got all up inside me, so I didn't.

"Soon as I finish this book, I've got my heart set on one called *Twig*, unless somebody already checked it out. Once, I tried reading more than one book at a time, but the stories started to get mixed up inside my head, so Mama told me just to read one at a time. That way, I won't get mixed up. You ever get mixed up?" she asked.

"Spoze everyone does sometimes."

"Yeah, I spoze."

"I'ma be a writer someday . . . did you know that?" Abigail asked.

"No."

"Well, I am . . . You just wait and see," she said.

"That's 'bout enough talkin', ain't it?" Meriwether asked. "Might be work out there for you, Gabriel, that needs doin'."

"Likely," I replied, and off I went, but the station was quiet and still.

One good thing about having nothing to do is that it gives you time to ponder, and as I waited idly at the gas pumps, that's exactly what I did. I thought about Abigail, though only ten, already seeming to know she was going to be a writer. Then I imagined Tink traveling the world, toting her camera, having her photographs printed on the pages of *National Geographic* and *Life* magazine. Suddenly, my thoughts flipped to Patrick, who seemed certain he had a future as a navy frogman. And Rosie Riley's path toward becoming a doctor seemed crystal clear too. How did they all seem so absolutely sure, when the thought of me becoming a pilot or even a detective somehow felt like questions instead of answers?

If Auntie Rita's claim about me having a special destiny was true, I asked myself exactly when and how I'd know what it was. Would it come straight at me like a fastball from a major-league baseball pitcher, leaving little doubt? Or maybe it would inch toward me slowly like a hairy caterpillar. Or perhaps it might come from out of the blue, like buckets of hail on a day it wasn't even supposed to rain, startling me unexpectedly.

CHAPTER 23

An hour later, half the folks in town who owned a car must have decided at the same time to show up at Jake's for gas and oil, with tires that were low on air and radiators that had decided to go haywire and all kinds of other automobile malfunctions. For the next two hours, Daddy, Matthew, Meriwether, and I didn't seem to get a minute of rest. Finally, things settled down.

Meriwether, with Abigail nestled beside him, was resting in the spot where he usually eats his lunch. "Now, that's what's called earnin' your pay," he told me. "'Bouta have our lunch now, nuthin' but fruit and turkey sandwiches.

You welcome to share. Abigail will pro'bly only eat half of hers."

"No, thank you. It'd ruin my appetite for supper, and Mama ain't fond of that."

"Suit yourself."

"I'll sit here a spell, though. Daddy's workin' on his ledger. Doesn't like to be bothered when it comes to numbers."

Meriwether patted the ground beside him and I took a seat. "How was that parade you were so excited about?"

"There were lots of people, and a marching band, and the mayor of Charleston gave a speech, and afterward there was a party at my cousin's house for my uncle Earl and some of the other war heroes. Never seen so many medals. And a photographer from the Charleston newspaper was there."

"Sounds like you had a very good time," he said.

"Boy, did I. Uncle Earl and the others told us all about the Battle of the Bulge. Said they'd never seen so much snow. Didn't know places on Earth could get that cold."

"They're right about that. It wasn't just cold—we were close to bein' frozen . . ." Suddenly, he stopped.

"What'd you say?" I asked him.

Abigail, whose nose had been buried in the book,

glanced over at her father. "You promised Mama not to talk about it 'round white folks . . . ever," she warned.

"Talk about what?"

Meriwether gazed off into space. "You good at keepin' secrets, Gabriel?"

"Usually."

Abigail stood up. "Don't tell him, Daddy. Mama made you swear on the Bible."

"I won't tell no one, I promise . . . What?"

"I hope you're a person of your word, Gabriel Haberlin."

"I am . . . Why'd you say that stuff about the Battle of the Bulge? You made it sound like you were there too."

"I was. And so were other colored men. And I'm tired of keepin' it bottled up inside me when y'all's soldiers get to brag and have fancy parades and all I have is a uniform, a Good Conduct Medal, an honorable discharge, and my memories. Always considered myself to be a brave man, but lately I've been so fulla fear, I've even stopped relivin' it with colored folks." He stared off again into the distance before continuing. "I already have the answer to this question, but lemme ask it anyway. Any colored soldiers honored in that parade?"

"No."

Meriwether drew his knees up to his chest and dropped his head into his hands. Abigail patted his shoulder tenderly. "Don't be sad about it again, Daddy."

"Startin' to feel like a dream," he whispered.

"What'd you do over there?"

He raised his head and looked straight at me. "I drove a tank."

"Wow!"

"Yessiree. I was a member of the United States Army's 761st Tank Battalion . . . all colored. Called ourselves the Black Panthers. Motto was Come Out Fighting, and that's exactly what we did. Proud to say we finished off a lotta Nazis and did our part to win the war."

"Wow!" I repeated. "That where you learned 'bout engines and all that?"

"Had some trainin' in high school but mastered it in the army. Spent more than a year learnin' everything 'bout those tanks, includin' how to take 'em apart and put 'em back together again. Most of us thought we'd never see any action. Idling in neutral same as a car, that's what it felt like. But we were prepared, ready, and rarin' to go . . . All we needed was someone to slip us into gear and step on the gas. Finally, General Patton did and we were deployed."

"So, you're a war hero just like my uncle," I told him.

"Sure thought I was 'til I was shipped home, got my discharge papers, and came face-to-face with the truth."

Right then, Matthew called out and waved me up front to the pumps to help him. I really didn't want the conversation to end because I had a lot of questions for Meriwether, but I had no choice. "Dang it! I gotta go."

"Remember the promise you made me."

The seriousness in his voice let me know how important it was to him, and I replied, "I will. I promise."

The next time I caught sight of him, he'd finished for the day. All I saw were their backs, his and Abigail's, as they walked away, Meriwether holding her hand. I wondered why he didn't want white folks to know about him being a tanker and what he meant by "the truth."

"G'night!" I hollered out.

They both turned and waved.

CHAPTER 24

As soon as I got to work the next day, I saw Abigail. And to my surprise, she was talking to Lucas, who, for some reason, was still hanging around. By the time I'd finished pumping gas and washing a car's windows, Lucas was driving off and Abigail was heading to the bathroom.

I was anxious to know what they'd been talking about, so I waited for her outside. Before long, she opened the door. I didn't even say hello, just began with a question. "What were you talkin' to Lucas about?"

"We weren't exactly talkin'. He was askin', I was answerin'."

"Askin' what?"

"What my name is. So I told him. Said he never knew anyone named Abigail b'fore. Then I told him it means 'a father's delight.' And I dunno why, but that made him laugh."

"Did you say anything to him about the bicycle?"

"No . . . not my place."

"Don't talk to him again," I commanded. "He ain't nice about colored people."

"Wasn't talkin' . . . like I told you," she said.

The questions I'd stored up from the previous day were begging to be answered, so I asked one. "Why doesn't your daddy want white folks to know 'bout him bein' in the army?"

She glanced toward the garage, where Meriwether was busy at work, before replying in a low voice, "Colored pastors all over been warnin' colored men who were in the service not to talk about it or show off in their uniforms."

"Why?"

"'Less they wanna wind up lynched from a tree or like that colored soldier over in Batesburg who got his eyes poked out and now he's forever blind. Would you want your daddy to be killed or forever blind?"

The thought made me shiver. "No."

"Neither do I. That's why you can't tell anyone. My

daddy and mama claim some white men don't take to the idea of a colored man bein' a war soldier equal to them."

When I'd gotten to work that day, I'd been determined to find out more about Mr. Hunter being a tanker. But Abigail had quickly turned my curiosity away from that and aimed it at the man she'd said had had his eyes poked out. Was she exaggerating the way kids sometimes do? Batesburg wasn't far off, and I hadn't heard anything about that. Then again, Mama and Daddy do their best to keep particularly gruesome news away from my ears. But I was twelve now, and like Meriwether said, practically a man in some places. I suppose I'd known for a while that the world, including Birdsong, USA, isn't always pretty, but recently my understanding of that was growing.

A car horn honking let me know a customer was waiting at the gas pumps, and since Matt was home sick with tonsillitis, I needed to skedaddle.

Daddy was there waiting, and he made it crystal clear that I had to stay up front so that when customers drove up, they didn't have to wait. "Not good for business," he instructed.

And that's exactly what I was doing the rest of the afternoon until a ruckus near the garage caught my attention. Meriwether was whooping and hollering.

"Lucas!" I proclaimed loudly, and ran like heck. But when I got to the garage, no one was there. Then I heard Meriwether shouting out back. I was awfully scared—until I laid eyes on them. Meriwether and Abigail were happy as could be, laughing out loud, jumping up and down. And soon I knew why. The hood of the '36 Chevy—the car that nobody could fix—was popped and the engine was purring like a kitten. Meriwether climbed inside the car and revved the motor. "Abigail, we own us an automobile!"

"I can't believe it," I told him. "No one else—"

Before I could finish, he cut me off. "What'd I tell you 'bout me, son?"

"That you're mighty good at fixin' things."

Abigail cracked a smile at me and ran her hand along the car from the front fender to the back. "My daddy is truly amazin', isn't he?"

"He sure is," I agreed. "Truly amazin'."

CHAPTER 25

If Meriwether getting that Chevy to run had surprised me, Daddy was practically in a state of disbelief.

"I'm plum flabbergasted, Meriwether. I swear you're some kinda magician." He turned to Abigail and asked, "Did you actually see your daddy fix it or did he wave a magic wand and say 'presto chango'?"

"Yessir, I saw him with my very own eyes. And all he was usin' were his tools. Plus, he doesn't even have a magic wand."

Daddy, Meriwether, and I cracked up.

Abigail squinted her eyes at my daddy. "You're just funnin' with me, huh?"

"I'll get the certificate of title transferred to your name soon as I can." Daddy motioned to the pile of papers on his desk. "It might take a little time, though, because as you can see, I'm swamped," he explained. "For now, I'll write a note in case of anything unforeseen." Daddy scribbled something on paper and handed it to Meriwether. "That should do for now."

"No hurry . . . and sir, all the backed-up cars are fixed, so seein' as Matthew's off sick, I'll spend the rest of my time helpin' Gabriel out front at the pump. Unless you got somethin' else that needs doin'."

"That'd be helpful to me, Meriwether"—Daddy glanced at his papers again—"and allow me to finish up here."

And so, Abigail, book in hand, happily skipped off to the garage to read while Meriwether and I worked.

Cheerfully, he greeted each customer, humming now and then. "Havin' a hard time believin' it. That I actually own me an automobile." He let out a joyful hoot.

"Told ya you would," I reminded him.

A smile parted his lips as he recalled the conversation we'd had. "That you did, didn't you? That you did."

After a spell, probably because the clouds had decided to give us a sprinkling of rain, the flow of customers came to a halt, so we found shelter and sat.

"I've been meanin' to ask you some questions," I told him.

He chuckled. "You mean start one of your interrogations?"

Most other times, a funny accusation like that would have made me grin, but because my thoughts were serious, I didn't. "It's just I was wonderin' about somethin' Abigail told me today—"

Meriwether interrupted me. "Abigail already confessed she told you why we try to keep quiet 'bout me havin' been in the army."

"Yessir . . . and also 'bout the man over in Batesburg who had his eyes poked out."

"That's a horrendous tale . . . Not sure it should be told to someone your age."

"But Abigail knows, and she's only ten."

His eyes lost their light. "Abigail's a southern colored girl . . . Some things havta be known by colored children for their safety. Mosta our young ones lose their innocence long before mosta y'all do."

"Still, if you don't mind, sir, I'd like to know."

"Got a thirst for knowledge . . . that it?"

"Yessir, spoze. I'm twelve now. Plus, I wanna know the truth."

"Sometimes the truth ain't pretty, Gabriel . . . Sometimes it's ugly."

"I'd like to know it just the same."

Meriwether stared off into the beyond and started talking. "Ever since we got back from overseas, me and my army buddies have been hearin' tales about colored soldiers who'd survived the war only to come home to the South and be murdered because of it. Wearin' a uniform made 'em sittin' ducks, and displayin' medals was much the same as wearin' a bull's-eye. Seems some white folks had trouble acceptin' that we colored soldiers not only had done our part but are as American as they are."

"And the man over in Batesburg?" I asked.

"Sergeant Isaac Woodard is his name. Happened back in February . . . Was still wearin' his uniform when he was pulled off the bus by the police. He was beaten and thrown in jail, had his eyes gouged out, and was denied appropriate medical attention."

"But why?"

"From what Pastor told us, the only crimes he committed were askin' to use the restroom, bein' a colored man, and bein' in a military uniform."

"But those aren't crimes," I said.

"Got one set of laws for us and another set for y'all,"

Meriwether said. "I can give you more truth if you're ready to swallow it. Most white folks in the South ain't, but you seem like you might be ready . . . You ready?"

"Think so."

"Half free ain't free. Bein' overseas gave us a taste of real freedom. And once we returned, havin' experienced that liberty made it hard to stomach not havin' it here . . . in the country we'd fought for, the country a lot of colored men gave their lives for. I realize that where we made our mistake was thinkin' it'd be better when we got home to places here in the South. Instead, in some ways it felt worse. It was as if the cruelty of Jim Crow had been multiplied. Can't do this . . . not allowed here. Bein' called a boy when what I am is a man. And look at the school my Abigail has to attend. How different is it from yours?"

Having already noticed this when I'd peered through the window into the colored school that day, I hung my head and said, "I know."

"Don't you be ashamed, son . . . Not like it's your doin'."

"Ain't right."

"Sorry, Mr. Gabriel . . . Be nice if the truth always tasted good, wouldn't it?"

"Yessir, it'd be mighty nice."

Right then, two cars pulled up at the same time.

"Suppose we have to end this serious conversation and earn our wage," he commented.

I half smiled at him. "Spoze so."

At closing time that evening, Daddy and I watched as Meriwether and Abigail climbed into their car. It was still raining off and on, but a full moon had appeared from behind the clouds, lighting up the night.

"Y'all will never know what this means to me. Thanks again," Meriwether told us.

Daddy gave a slight nod of his head. "You're welcome."

"See ya tomorrow," I said.

"But not me," Abigail informed us. "My mama'll be home tonight. Just wait 'til she sees our car. Bye-bye, Gabriel and Mr. Jake."

As they drove off, I watched as the Chevy's headlights made the wet street glisten and the red taillights got smaller and smaller until they finally turned the corner and were gone. But the truth I'd learned that day was whirling around like a spinning top inside my head.

CHAPTER 26

There are things you shouldn't be worried about when your punishment is at long last over and you finally get to ride your bicycle again—things like whether your bicycle will get stolen too or whether Betty Babcock might come barreling at you again in her yellow Roadmaster. But those were exactly the things that were on my mind as I rode my bicycle to work. As I'd promised Mama and Daddy, I obeyed every safety law, looked both ways before I pedaled across intersections, and, most importantly, stopped at red lights. Sheriff Hector Monk sailed by me in his patrol car and waved.

Thankfully, Matt was back at work when I arrived. Before helping him, I took my bicycle inside.

"Hi, Mr. Hunter," I said. "I'ma park this inside the garage, if that's all right with you," I told him.

He rose up from the hood of the car where his head had been buried. "In case the bicycle thief makes a return visit?"

"Yessir, considerin' what happened to yours."

"Be glad to keep my eyes on it and my ears alert. You're bein' mighty safe on it now, ain't you?"

"Awfully safe."

He smiled. "Glad to know that. I would hate to have anything bad happen to a friend."

"Friend? Thank you, sir."

"I bet I know what you're thinkin' . . . but age has little to do with genuine friendship. Recipe for friendship is liking and trust. Respect gets mixed up in there too."

I thought for a minute about Tink being one of my best friends and replied, "That sounds right," parked the Schwinn in the corner, and headed off to do my work.

Matthew looked practically good as new, eyes clear and blue, and together we manned the station. He was finally letting me check the oil without him watching over me, and I was getting the hang of the tire pressure gauge too.

The sun was shining, and for an August day in Birdsong, it wasn't too hot since the wind was blowing just enough.

Daddy was on the car lot, and it looked like he was about to make a sale. I was glad, because the night before, he'd promised Mama and me a weekend trip to Hilton Head if he did.

WHAT HAPPENED THAT evening began to convince me that Meriwether had really meant it when he'd called me his friend.

I was returning tools to the garage when I saw him. As usual, he was taking his lunch break, sitting propped against the wall.

"You in a hurry?" he asked.

"No. Kinda slow today. Plus, Matthew's back."

"Good. I have something to show you," Meriwether said as he pulled out his wallet.

Wondering what it could be, I quickly settled in beside him.

"Picture of me and my tank crew in the 761st right

before we got deployed," he explained, and presented a black-and-white snapshot.

Five smiling colored soldiers in uniform stood beside a tank.

Meriwether's face beamed. "That's an M4 Sherman tank."

I examined each face until I picked him out and pointed. "This is you, huh?"

"Yes indeed. You have a good eye."

"Who are the others?"

One by one he identified them. "This man here was our commander. We called him Mozart, because whenever he had a break, his lips were on his harmonica, composin', he said . . . Real name was Emmanuel Bowman, outta Denver, Colorado. The one salutin' was a college boy named Vernon Morse from New Orleans, our ammunition loader. We called him Doc 'cause that's what he aimed to be someday. Was all set to enter Meharry Medical College in Nashville but got drafted." Meriwether's eyes filled with water, but he didn't cry. "He lost an arm and leg . . . and all his dreams. Of course, that there is me. I was the driver."

"What'd they call you?"

"They called me Meri. Used to tease me with that

kids' nursery rhyme . . . 'Mary Had a Little Lamb.' And this here is Fred Ratner, the gunner . . . We called him Rat for short. He was from Los Angeles. Died instantly right in front of me out there in the Ardennes Forest. We lost him and Mozart during the same battle on the same day." He hesitated before continuing. "And that smilin' fella is Charlie Denton, my co-driver. He was born in Alabama . . . Nicknamed him Custard on account of him havin' yella skin.

"Charlie's settled up in Michigan now, workin' at the Ford automobile plant. Always after me to join him. Says he'll have a job waitin' for me. My wife, though, she's not fond of the cold, and besides that, she has her church work here," he remarked.

Meriwether Hunter studied the picture again and sighed. "Had some good times with those men, and, of course, very hard ones too. One thing I can honestly say about all of us: we were proud to serve our country."

Right then, Patrick startled us. "Hey, y'all. Whatcha lookin' at?"

We'd been so focused on the photograph, neither of us had heard him approach.

Hurriedly, Meriwether slipped the photo into the

pocket of his coveralls. "Nuthin' you'd be interested in," he said as he stood and headed back to the garage. In his haste, he'd left a ripe peach sitting on top of his lunch bag.

Patrick, noticing the peach, called out, "Hey, uncle!" Then, remembering how I felt about him calling all colored men *uncle*, he glanced my way and asked, "What's his name again?"

"Mr. Meriwether Hunter."

"Hey, Mr. Meriwether Hunter . . . if you're not gonna eat this peach, can I have it?"

Meriwether poked his head out of the garage. "Yes, Patrick."

"Thank you."

"Welcome."

Patrick walked alongside me to the front of the station. "If you're wonderin' what I'm doin' here . . . truth is I didn't have nuthin' else to do," he said between taking bites from the peach. "Plus, my daddy said a grease monkey—that's the same thing as a mechanic—is a good thing to be and I oughtta be over here learnin' as much as I can even if I'm not gettin' paid for it. And he also claims that just 'cuz your heart's set on somethin', like mine is on becomin' a navy frogman, doesn't mean it's gonna really come true, so it'd be smart to learn somethin' else if I can . . . and bein' a mechanic is that somethin' else. Whatcha think 'bout that?"

"I think it's time for you to talk to my daddy."

"Mornings okay with you?" Daddy asked him, when Patrick blurted out his proposal.

Patrick tugged on his swim goggles. "Sure. I spoze swimmin' could wait 'til the afternoon."

"Good—you can hitch a ride with me."

And that was how Patrick Kelly became the unpaid apprentice mechanic at Jake's and how he came to be with us that morning when the mostly right-side-up world of mostly quiet Birdsong, USA, for a while turned upside down.

CHAPTER 27

It was after ten p.m. on Sunday, but someone was leaning on the doorbell and banging on our front door. I leaped out of bed.

"What in kingdom come!" Daddy fussed. Mama and Daddy were already in their nightclothes.

It was Meriwether, breathing fast, his eyes red and looking wild. In my daddy's language, he was all fueled up. "It was him! I know it! Tried to kill my girl," he hollered. "Tried to kill my girl!"

"Who?" Daddy asked.

"Lucas!"

"Is Abigail hurt?" Daddy asked.

"No, she's fine . . . over at the church with my wife, Pastor, and some of our men, keepin' watch, just in case."

"Come inside and have a seat, Mr. Hunter," Mama softly beckoned.

Somewhat reluctantly, he stepped over the threshold into the house, but instead of sitting, he paced.

"Tell me," Daddy said.

"A few hours ago, just this evenin', we got home from a special church service in Charleston. I parked our car out back and we came in through the rear door. After a while, Abigail notices what looks like a gift on the front porch. 'Daddy, look. There's a box,' she says. And I figured 'cause last week was her birthday, someone from the church musta left it for her as a surprise, you know. So I tell her to go on and get it. And she goes out to the porch. 'It's for me,' she says. 'Got my name on it. Abigail, A Father's Delight,' and me and Phoebe are smilin' and I tell her go ahead and open it . . . not thinkin' 'til she calls out, 'Somethin' inside the box is movin' around,' and just as I get outside, she gets the box open . . . and it strikes at her, missin' her by no more than a few inches."

"What?" I asked.

"A diamondback rattlesnake."

Mama let out a gasp. "Lord, no!"

"Lucky for me there was a shovel close by, which I grabbed and jammed into its neck."

"You kill it?" Daddy asked.

"With one blow."

"And what has you convinced it was Lucas? How would he know your girl's name and what it meant?" Daddy questioned.

I answered, "'Cuz he asked her and she told him. I saw him talkin' to her."

"Abigail claimed the same thing, but there's something else. This was in the box too. Knew I'd lost it somewhere the other day after I'd shown it to Gabriel. Now I figure it fell outta my coveralls in the garage and Lucas musta found it." It was the picture of Meriwether and his tank crew. "Had to be him, I tell you. Had to be."

"You talk to the sheriff?"

Meriwether locked eyes with Daddy. "For what? Got no proof. B'sides, even if there'd been a witness, colored folk accusin' a white man would only likely bring me and mine more trouble."

"But Hector Monk's reasonable and a good sheriff," Mama claimed.

Meriwether turned his gaze to her. "Not aimin' to disrespect you, ma'am, especially in your own house, but the way my people see it, like most sheriffs in these parts, he appears to belong to y'all. Colored people 'round here, we got nuthin' to protect us but our wits, and sometimes even those fail us. Now and then, the good Lord takes over."

"But a child's involved. It hasta be reported to the authorities. What if she'd been killed?" Mama argued.

"If she'd been killed, it's likely I wouldn't be here talkin' to y'all . . . I'd be—" Abruptly he stopped and took a deep breath. "Gotta be careful what I say in case y'all wind up under oath in a court of law, don't I?"

Daddy pleaded with him, "Promise me, Meriwether, that you won't take the law into your own hands."

Meriwether opened his hands and stared at his palms. "Been keepin' promises all my life—promised to be loyal to my country and bravely serve, which I did. And for the most part, I've even kept the Ten Commandments 'cept for the one that forbids us to covet . . . Hard for a colored man to see some of y'all havin' what looks like heaven on earth and not long for it myself." His tears began flowing. "I've been a good man, mostly kind. As honest as this life would let me be." He hunched his shoulders. "Would think this would be a sweet place, named the way it is.

But even a good colored man can't be a real man in this town called Birdsong."

The fire that'd been in him minutes earlier when he'd rung our doorbell had completely vanished. And my daddy, Jake Haberlin, embraced him as Mr. Meriwether Hunter sobbed.

CHAPTER 28

"It's attempted murder!" I told them after Meriwether left. "Lucas can't just get away with it. You gotta
do something. She's just a little girl. At least you gotta
fire him!"

"Go on to bed . . . This was not for your eyes and ears,"
Daddy said.

"Why . . . 'cuz it's the truth?" I asked.

"No, 'cause you're just a boy."

"Am not . . . In some places, I'd practically be a man."

"This ain't some places, this is Birdsong, South
Carolina, and in Birdsong, South Carolina, you're still a
child. I'll handle this."

Standing right in front of him, almost eye to eye, I glared. "Hope so."

"Go on to bed now, b'fore this turns into something it shouldn't," Daddy commanded.

Mama patted my shoulder. "Go on, Gabriel. G'night."

"It ain't right and it ain't fair, and don't tell me it's just the ways of the South. Y'all ever figure the ways of the South are wrong? Y'all ever figure the ways of the South need changin'? Y'all ever figure—"

"That's enough for right now, Gabriel. We're all tired. Got a workday tomorrow and now all this," Daddy said with a sigh. "G'night."

Hours later, I was still wide awake, staring into the darkness, questions coming at me, one after the other, unable to find answers.

Was it because of the picture and finding out about Meriwether being a tanker that had made Lucas do it, or had he been planning this all along? Unless he confessed, there was no way to know. Nothing about this was fair or just. How could it be that a man can't protect his family— and even feared going to the sheriff?

One thing I was certain of was this: if Lucas had had even a sprinkling of Meriwether's goodness, I'd be sleeping soundly right now. How could anyone do such a thing?

Over and over again, I pictured Abigail, the diamondback striking at her with its fangs prepared to deliver its deadly venom, and the image made my body quiver.

FINALLY, I DOZED off, and it was well after sunrise when the sound of Patrick's voice outside woke me up. "Gabriel! Gabriel! You awake? I'm here to ride to work with your daddy."

I parted the curtains and motioned him to the back door. And that was when the front doorbell rang again. Daddy, already up and dressed, beat me to the door. Mama trailed him.

I expected to see Meriwether again, but this time it was Sheriff Monk and his deputy, J. J. Carroway. Because everything about the sheriff was round, especially his belly, and J. J. was a slender man, whenever they were side by side, I couldn't help but be reminded of Laurel and Hardy.

"Mornin', Sheriff, J. J."

"Mornin', Jake . . . Agatha."

As soon as Patrick saw them, he joked, "What's wrong? Someone get murdered or somethin'?"

Sheriff Monk glanced from Patrick to me and said,

"We came to have a private talk with your daddy 'n' mama."

"In other words, you want me and Gabriel to scram, huh?" Patrick asked.

The sheriff nodded, and I thought I saw a hint of a smile on J. J. Carroway's lips.

"If it's about Meriwether and Lucas, I wanna stay," I told Daddy.

"Did they finally have a fight?" Patrick asked. "'Cuz that day when Lucas spit tobacco on his foot, it sure looked like they were 'bout to, remember?"

That comment seemed to turn on a light inside Sheriff Monk. He and J. J. shared a look. "The boys can stay," he decided.

Of course, Mama welcomed everyone to the dining room table and offered the men coffee, which they accepted.

"What can I help you gentlemen with?" Daddy asked.

"Not sure I'm a gentleman, Jake, and I know for certain J. J. ain't, but that aside, we're here to ask y'all a few questions 'bout a visit I got first thing this mornin' at the office from Miss Felicity Duval."

"Felicity Duval?" Daddy asked.

"Found her on my doorstep at six a.m. Said she had

a story to tell 'bout somethin' disturbin' to her that went on last night on The Other Side . . . with a colored family. Claims someone left a box on the porch for the family's li'l gal and that the box contained a large diamondback rattler. Not sure how she got hold of it, but she brought me the thing in a potato sack, includin' the chopped-off head."

"It was dead, of course," J. J. commented as he stirred the coffee Mama had given him.

"A diamondback? They's deadly!" Patrick exclaimed.

"Anyhow, seems Miss Duval gives piano lessons to the gal, name is . . ." He reached into his pocket, pulled out a wad of papers, and searched.

"Abigail," Daddy told him. "Girl's name is Abigail."

"Like I was sayin', Miss Duval gives her piano lessons now and then, and she's fond of her and was quite upset about this incident with the diamondback."

"You said you had questions, Hector . . . and I need to get to work," Daddy said.

"And me too," Patrick added. "I need to get to work with him. I'm an apprentice mechanic now."

The sheriff cleared his throat. "Just wanna know if you have any ideas who the responsible party might be."

As if to warn me not to speak, Mama gently squeezed my shoulder. "Didn't Miss Duval say?" she asked.

"No ma'am. That seemed to be the one bit of information she was lackin', which was a surprise to me, because generally she seems to know folks' business even b'fore they know it themselves." The sheriff gave a grim smile.

"If the snake didn't bite her, isn't it still attempted murder because that's what was intended?" I asked.

"You'd be best to try and sell more cars, Jake. Think you might have to send this boy to law school," J. J. said.

"Y'all certain you don't have any clues about who might have done such a thing?" Sheriff Monk asked again. "Like to be able to give an answer to Miss Duval and to the colored pastor if he comes callin', which I'm sure he will."

"You talked to Meriwether yet?" my daddy asked.

"No . . . Planned to talk to him sometime this afternoon. Thought I'd stop here first b'fore talkin' to the boy . . . you know, get your impression of things."

"Can't bring myself to accuse a man without proof," Daddy answered.

With that, Sheriff Hector Monk took a big gulp of coffee, pushed away from the table, and stood up. "I'd like to thank you fine folks for your time and good coffee," he said as he headed for the door. But before he and J. J. reached the door, he stopped in his tracks and turned to Daddy. "Got one more question for you, Jake."

"What's that?"

"Lucas and this boy, Meriwether, would you say they get along?"

Daddy replied with his own question. "How well do you know Lucas, Hector?"

"Well enough."

"Then you already have the answer to your question."

CHAPTER 29

No sooner had the sheriff and J. J. left than Daddy announced he was going to stop at Meriwether's on his way to work.

"I'm comin' too. He's *my* friend," I said.

As if searching for her approval, he gazed at Mama, and apparently he found it. "Get dressed in a hurry," he instructed me.

"And don't forget 'bout me, Mr. Haberlin," Patrick reminded him. "It's my first day of learnin' to be an unpaid apprentice mechanic, remember?"

Patrick's words made Mama smile. Normally something like that would have caused my daddy to grin as well, but his face was awash with worry, and he simply nodded.

The radio was off, the front car windows were rolled down, and the morning air was already warm. Patrick was in the back seat whistling. Birdsong was just waking up.

"Y'all remember the house?" Daddy asked.

"It's on Holly Street. I forget the address but I know the one," I answered.

In no time flat we were parked in front of Meriwether's house. "Be right back," Daddy said.

But I already had one foot out the door. I wondered if he was going to try to stop me, but he didn't. Of course, Patrick was on my heels.

We'd just stepped onto the sidewalk leading up to the house when two colored men who'd been sitting in porch chairs on each side of the door rose to their feet.

"What can we do for y'all?" one of the men asked.

"Here to see Meriwether Hunter," Daddy replied.

Both men's faces were sour, and they exchanged a strange look before one of them said, "Y'all got business with him?"

"He works for me."

"Wait here," one of the men commanded, and when

he went inside, the other man stood in front of the door as if he were guarding it.

Seconds later, the colored pastor, whom I recognized from the station when he came to get gas, was on the porch. "They're okay," he informed the men.

Then he said, "Good mornin', Mr. Haberlin."

"Mornin', Pastor Honeywell."

Daddy and the pastor extended hands, and they shook.

"I'd like you to meet two pastors, one outta Charleston, the other from Orangeburg—friends of mine from divinity school, Pastor Baldwin and Pastor Ellison. Pastors, this is Jake Haberlin . . . He's a decent man . . . owner of the gas station here that's listed in *The Green Book*."

"*The Green Book*?" one pastor repeated, then finally smiled.

"Nice to meet you, Mr. Haberlin," the other said.

"This is my boy, Gabriel, and his friend Patrick."

"Pleased to meet y'all too," the pastors responded with slight nods of their heads.

"Pleased to meet you as well," I told them.

"As well," Patrick uttered.

"We're here to watch over our folk," Pastor Honeywell revealed as he scanned the street. The front door was opened, we were ushered inside, and quickly it was shut and locked.

Phoebe, Meriwether's wife, greeted us. A handkerchief was in her hand and her eyes had that just-cried look. "Mornin', Mr. Haberlin, Gabriel." But when she reached Patrick, she stalled.

"Patrick," he informed her.

"Mornin'," she said softly.

And we replied, "Mornin', ma'am."

On one side of the room, I noticed open suitcases partially packed.

Suddenly, Abigail whirled into the room. "What y'all doin' here so early in the mornin'? If you came to see the snake, you're too late, 'cuz Miss Duval already came and got it. And I wasn't scared, in case that's what you were wonderin', but you shoulda seen the way my daddy killed it so quick. And another thing . . . One day I'm gonna write my very own book about Birdsong, includin' y'all and everything that happened, but mostly it's gonna be 'bout my daddy drivin' a tank durin' the war so that way it won't be a secret anymore, and even though he didn't get a parade, everyone'll still know how brave he was."

"That's a ton of words to come outta someone all at once, Abigail," Pastor Honeywell commented.

A grinning Abigail, who'd obviously considered it a compliment, replied, "Thank you, Pastor."

"Your daddy drove a tank . . . a real tank . . . in the war?" Patrick asked.

Abigail replied, "Yes."

But when Patrick opened his mouth to say something else, I gave him a warning nudge and he knew to be quiet.

Abigail's eyes then landed on her mama. She shrugged and apologized. "Sorry, Mama, but I figure since we're leavin' Birdsong today, it doesn't matter anymore if folks 'round here know 'bout Daddy and the tanks."

Daddy glanced toward the suitcases and asked Phoebe, "Y'all leavin' today?"

"Yessir, we're goin' north to Michigan. A fella Meri was in the service with has been after him to come north. Claims he can get him a job in no time at the Ford plant, and we'll have a better future there. Hope he's right."

"Considerin' what happened, can't say I blame you," my father told her. Then he inquired, "Where's Meriwether now?"

The pastor responded, "Don't know. He drove off just b'fore you got here. Said he'd be back shortly. Claimed he had to talk to someone about an important matter. I assumed he was referring to you."

"Lucas," I blurted.

"Y'all ain't gotta worry. I heard him when he promised Mama not to hurt him. She even made him swear on the Bible," Abigail revealed.

Tears rolled down Phoebe's face. "Nuthin' I could say to stop him . . . Nuthin'." Her hand clenched the handkerchief, and right then she reminded me of my own mama.

The next thing I knew, Daddy told us, "C'mon!" and headed for the door.

Pastor Honeywell rushed outside with us, whispered something to his two friends, and followed us to the car. "I'm comin' with y'all. Got an obligation to every member of my flock, and Meriwether's one of 'em."

And together, we sped to the station.

CHAPTER 30

Patrick leaned toward me and did something he rarely did—whispered. "You think Meriwether's gonna kill Lucas?"

"He swore on the Bible," I reminded him.

"Then maybe Lucas's gonna kill him."

Upon hearing those words, Daddy said, "Patrick, that's enough back there, you hear?"

"Yessir."

Pastor Honeywell bowed his head and softly prayed.

The quiet allowed a notion to enter my mind: The first time you meet someone, it's the beginning of a brand-new unmapped trail, so there's no way of knowing if that path is going to be a short one, a long one, or somewhere in between, or maybe one that takes you in a circle and therefore never ends. Not much time had passed since the day I'd met Meriwether, but because he was so interesting and kind, I didn't want our friendship to be over yet. But like it or not, it appeared we were close to the end of our road.

I glanced over at Patrick and wondered if ours would be a forever trail. Probably.

Daddy's driving that day reminded me of the day I'd ridden with Betty Babcock—careless, seeming as if we were flying.

As soon as we careered around the corner to the station, I saw it: the black '36 Chevy, Meriwether's car.

As soon as our wheels stopped rolling, I opened the door to get out and fell flat onto the asphalt.

"Gabriel!" Daddy yelled.

I sprang up and sprinted to the garage. And there they were. Lucas was backed up against the wall, and Meriwether was holding a metal pipe up high, prepared to strike. "Meriwether! Don't!" I hollered.

"Not gonna hurt him . . . Just want him to admit it was him who did it."

I inched inside.

And right then, Daddy, Pastor Honeywell, and Patrick arrived.

"Meriwether," Daddy said calmly, and started to walk toward him.

"Y'all stand down! This is between me and him!" Meriwether warned.

I sidestepped closer.

Meriwether noticed and told me, "You too, Gabriel."

"Put the pipe down, Meriwether. No good's gonna come of this. By God's grace, Abigail wasn't hurt," the pastor pleaded.

Lucas smirked. "So, father's li'l delight ain't dead. What a shame."

Meriwether glanced at me, and I knew from the look in his eyes that the promise he'd made to his wife was about to be broken.

I'm close enough, I thought as I charged him. The force was just enough to make Meriwether lose his balance and drop the pipe.

For a few seconds, everything was calm.

Then Lucas suddenly howled out, sounding like a sick hound. We watched as he clutched his chest and slumped to the garage floor.

Daddy went to check him. "Lucas?" He shook his shoulder. "Lucas?"

But Lucas wouldn't budge. His eyes were wide open, staring, lifeless.

Many moments of silence passed. The pastor bowed his head in prayer.

"He's dead, ain't he?" Patrick finally said.

"Appears so," Daddy commented.

"But Meriwether didn't even touch him. So why'd he die?" Patrick asked.

"Dunno," Daddy replied. "Dunno."

For a while no one moved or spoke any words unless you count what was being said with our eyes—mostly disbelief.

Finally, Meriwether leaned against a car inside the garage, and Pastor Honeywell joined him and placed an arm around his shoulder.

Patrick headed over to Lucas and stared. "Seen dead critters b'fore but never a dead man . . . Looks peculiar, don't he? Heard of people just droppin' dead, but never believed it 'til just now."

I really didn't want to get near Lucas, but I figured this might be the only time I was going to be this close to a dead person, so I went over and stood beside Patrick and studied the eyes of what used to be Lucas Shaw. His body was still there, but his soul was gone. I supposed if he'd been a good person, I would have cried, but seeing as he wasn't, not a single tear came.

"That's enough now," Daddy said. "I'm gonna go call Doc Riley."

"For what? Doc Riley ain't Jesus . . . cain't raise him from the dead," Patrick declared.

"To determine what killed him," Daddy answered. "And to take care of his body."

CHAPTER 31

"Doc's on his way," Daddy told us. He'd covered the body of Lucas Shaw with a blanket, and we'd gathered outside the garage.

"God surely works in mysterious ways," Pastor Honeywell said. "And in this case, expeditiously. Wouldn't you agree, Mr. Haberlin?" he inquired.

"I sure would."

"So there's likely no need for you to call the sheriff. Would you agree with that as well?" the pastor added.

"No crime was committed," I said.

"Woulda been, if it hadn't been for Gabriel," Patrick noted.

Meriwether sighed. "Spoze we're even now. I saved you from bein' hit by that car, and now you turned 'round and saved me from"—he hesitated before continuing—"killin' a man. What you think 'bout that, my young friend?" He cracked a smile.

I grinned. "I think it's just fine, and now that Lucas is dead, y'all don't have to move, do you?"

Meriwether and the pastor shared a look. "I'm 'bout done with Birdsong, and I have a strong suspicion Birdsong is through with me . . . Time to head north to a place that's rumored to be a trifle more hospitable."

"What's that mean, *hospitable*?" I asked.

"Welcoming," he answered.

"I think it'll be better for y'all up there too," Daddy said.

"Only one way to know and that's to find out for myself."

"Now, about the sheriff?" Pastor Honeywell inquired again.

"Like Gabriel said, no crime's been committed, so I can't say I see a reason for me to call him, but y'all should be aware that he did come 'round my house this mornin' askin' 'bout the snake. Seems Miss Duval carried it over to him and he was fulla questions. Thissa small town"—he glanced at Patrick—"and tales fly fast."

The pastor chuckled. "Birdsong's a fittin' name, then, ain't it?"

"That it is."

Old Pastor Honeywell stared long and hard into my daddy's eyes. "If you don't have any objections, Mr. Haberlin, I think it'd be wise for Meriwether not to be here right 'bout now. So we're gonna head on back to the house to check on Phoebe and Abigail."

"That'd be wise of you."

Meriwether reached for Daddy's hand and they shook. "Thank you, Mr. Haberlin. It's likely I'll see y'all b'fore we leave."

"I'm sure of that, Meriwether. Plus, you'll need those title and registration papers for the car. I'm expecting them in today's mail."

Meriwether smiled. "Thanks again, Mr. Haberlin, for everything."

"Jake . . . The name's Jake."

Then Meriwether turned to me and said, "And thank you, Gabriel."

"Welcome," I replied. "And thank you too for . . . you know, that day with the bicycle. Sure are a lot of thank-yous around here!"

"I know."

"Bye, Mr. Meriwether Hunter," Patrick uttered.

"So long," Meriwether replied.

And together, Meriwether and the pastor headed to the car. Pastor's arm was around his shoulder, reminding me of a father with his son.

CHAPTER 32

Daddy sent Patrick and me outside to work, and I was filling a tank with gas when an odd thought popped into my mind. The same way a car stops when it's out of fuel or something goes haywire in the engine, Lucas had come to his end. But unlike cars and other machines, once our light goes out, there's no way to ever start us up again.

"You see his eyes?" Patrick asked. "Hope I don't have nightmares."

"Don't remind me."

Cars rolled in and out as if it was a regular day and Lucas wasn't lying dead inside the station.

A short while later, Doc Riley drove up with his daughter Rosie beside him.

He politely greeted everyone, and everyone returned his greeting.

"He's in the garage," my daddy told him.

Rosie glanced at Patrick and me, said, "Hi, y'all," and took out a notebook and pencil and began writing.

"Hi, Rosie."

"How'd he die?" she asked.

"Just dropped, same as a peach from a tree, and died," Patrick answered.

Rosie jotted something in her notebook, and together we trailed her daddy and mine into the garage.

Doc Riley lifted the blanket from Lucas. "Jake, you said he was clutchin' his chest?"

Daddy nodded.

"And cried out in pain?"

"Yes."

"Howled is more like it," Patrick added.

Rosie peeked at the body but didn't even flinch.

Doc Riley scratched his head, covered Lucas back up, and said, "So, Lucas Shaw's luck finally ran out."

"Huh?" Daddy asked.

"His heart. It was why the army, navy, and marines wouldn't take him when he tried to enlist. Wondered when it was finally gonna quit on him . . . Just a matter of time. Even the heart doctor I sent him to down in Charleston was in total agreement. Born with it, you know . . . a sick ticker. Nuthin' could be done. His sister won't likely ask for an autopsy, with his medical history. I'll stop over there to deliver the news and call the undertaker."

Rosie, who'd been busily taking notes, stopped and asked, "Did rigor mortis set in yet, Daddy?"

"No, Rosie—takes at least four hours, remember?"

She nodded and scribbled something else in her tablet.

"My Rosie's got her mind set on becomin' a doctor, you know."

"Jake?" a voice called from outside the garage. "Jake?" Suddenly, Sheriff Monk and J. J. showed up in the doorway.

"Lucas croaked!" Patrick blurted.

The sheriff and J. J. glanced at each other, then stepped quickly over to the body.

Doc Riley lifted the blanket to show the sheriff and J. J. "Heart finally gave out. Surprised it lasted him this long."

The sheriff and J. J. stared at the body as if they didn't believe what they were seeing.

"Lucas Shaw done gone and died?" J. J. asked.

"Dropped dead right in front of us," Daddy told him.

Sheriff Monk tugged at his earlobe, ran his hand across his brow, and glanced around at each one of us before he asked Doc Riley, "No sign of injury of any kind?"

"Not a thing."

Sheriff Monk's face twisted with questions and then he asked Daddy, "Where's that colored boy who works here?"

"Home, I'd suppose."

With the gentlest nudge possible, I let Patrick know to be quiet. And thankfully, he was.

"You notify his sister yet, Doc?"

"I was going to, and then call Billy McGinty to come pick up the body."

"And you're certain it was his heart?"

"I sent him to the specialist in Charleston myself. Remember after Pearl Harbor when he couldn't enlist? Was because of that."

Sheriff Hector Monk gazed up at the ceiling, sighed deeply, then proclaimed, "Doc, I know you to be an honest fella. I'll stop by the Shaw place for you, save you the trip."

"Thank you kindly. Got some house calls to make."

A car honked out at the station pumps three times. "If

y'all don't mind," Daddy told them, "I'll excuse myself . . .
Customer's waitin'."

J. J. Carroway shook his head in disbelief. "Cain't hardly
believe it. Lucas Shaw really done gone and dropped dead."

The sheriff nervously tugged his ear again, and I
watched as doubt returned to his eyes. But seconds later, a
shrug of his shoulders made it appear as if the investigation
was over.

The waiting car honked again, and Daddy hurried off.

Patrick and I watched from the doorway as the
sheriff and J. J. climbed into their patrol car. And when
Sheriff Hector Monk spoke into the car's two-way radio,
I knew that the news of Lucas Shaw's death was about to
be broadcast all over Birdsong, USA.

Doc Riley used the phone in Daddy's office to call
Billy McGinty, the mayor-undertaker, and then he and
pretty Rosie Riley were gone too. She carried his black
doctor's bag as if it already belonged to her.

Before long, Mama showed up, wearing her most
worried look. "Y'all all right?" she asked Patrick and me.

"You wanna see him?" Patrick asked her. "I gotta warn
you, though, his eyes is wide open . . . so it's even scarier
than a Dracula movie."

Mama closed her eyes and shook her head. "Horrible thing for y'all boys to witness."

Because so many things that summer seemed to be pushing me to the finish line of childhood, I wanted to say, I'm not a boy anymore. But because it didn't seem to be the right time for that, I didn't. She placed her hand on my shoulder.

Patrick lifted the Saint Christopher necklace from underneath his shirt and nervously fingered the small round medal. Mama, taking note, said to him, "I can drive you home, Patrick, if you like. It's been quite a day."

"No, thank you, ma'am. I'ma go up front and help out Mr. Haberlin, like it was agreed," he replied. Then, his hand tightly clutching his medal, he sauntered off.

"Daddy told me everything when he phoned me," Mama said. "And that Meriwether's leavin' town today with his family."

"Yeah, headin' north, clear to Michigan. He claims Birdsong's 'bout done with him."

Mama gazed off toward the foothills. "Odd the way lives crisscross down here. I'm happy he's heading north. But I'll be forever grateful for him bein' here that day when the car almost hit you . . . forever grateful."

"Me too. He sure is a true friend."

A half hour passed before Billy McGinty arrived in his black hearse. "Sad day it is, Agatha and Jake, when the Lord takes someone as young as Lucas Shaw . . . Sad day indeed."

Daddy, Mama, Patrick, and I glanced at one another, and Patrick said what we were probably all thinking. "He wasn't very nice."

No one disagreed, not even Billy McGinty.

"I reckon his time had come," Daddy added.

"Bad heart, Doc Riley said. Never knew . . . You?"

"He never said a word to me 'bout it."

Minutes later, Daddy and Billy loaded the lifeless body of Lucas Shaw into the back of the Cadillac hearse.

"It never stops amazin' me how heavy a dead body can be. Y'all take care, now," the mayor-undertaker said as he turned the key in the ignition. Nothing happened but a clicking noise, and he had to turn it again before it finally started. "I'll bring it in for service next week, Jake."

"Might havta wait on that . . . Got no mechanic now."

"Still got that colored boy, don't ya?"

"No. He's leavin' for a job up north."

"Thatsa shame. I been hearin' folks 'round town braggin' on him."

"Yes, it's a shame."

More goodbye words were uttered and we stood together, staring at the funeral car as it made its way down the street.

Lucas Shaw was really gone—for good.

CHAPTER 33

That night, our house was mostly quiet. Mama didn't even offer up her usual dinnertime small talk. The windows were open and the radio was off, but outside, crickets were creating music and lightning bugs were making their nightly summertime appearance. The tick of the grandfather clock seemed louder than usual.

"You think he left already?" I asked as I helped with the dishes.

"Dunno," Daddy replied. "Hope not. I have those car papers for him."

"What if he forgot?"

"Not likely. Havin' those papers is pretty crucial, especially since he won't likely be back anytime soon."

"Can we drive over there and see?"

He folded up the newspaper. "It's mighty important to you, isn't it, Gabriel?"

"Yessir, it is."

And before I knew it, the windows had been closed, and we, including Mama, were inside the car, headed to Meriwether's house.

"His car's still there!" I exclaimed as we drove up. I was so happy, I wanted to cry.

The two pastors were still there too, but they smiled as soon as they saw us. "Evenin', Pastors," Daddy said. "This is my wife, Agatha."

"Evenin', ma'am," they replied.

We were all standing on the porch when Meriwether opened the door. His wife, Phoebe, and Abigail huddled in close beside him. Pastor Honeywell stood behind them.

"We were just comin' to see y'all, but y'all got here first, huh?" Abigail said.

Meriwether grinned, opened the screen door, and welcomed us inside.

"Gabriel was worried that you'd already left," Mama explained.

"Would never leave town without sayin' goodbye to friends," he replied.

"Before I forget," Daddy told him as he reached into his pocket, "got those title papers for the car in your name, and the registration."

Meriwether took the papers, examined them, and smiled. "Ain't this somethin'."

"Wanna thank y'all for everything," Phoebe said. "Our time here has ended sooner than expected and certainly not in the way we'd planned, but Birdsong has some fine folks."

"My wife is right. Thank you, Jake, for the opportunity you gave me . . . and for the automobile." Meriwether patted my shoulder before continuing, "Gabriel's very much like you . . . kindhearted and respectful. Y'all have a right to be mighty proud. And sorry to leave you so sudden-like without another mechanic, but Pastor says it's likely when word gets out about me bein' at the garage when Lucas died, there's bound to be trouble."

"I'll make out fine . . . Might even be able to lure the fella who went up to Raleigh to come back. Word is his romance didn't work out," Daddy told him.

Pastor looked at his watch. "Hate to interrupt such pleasant farewells, but it's 'bout that time. Y'all got your *Green Book*, Phoebe? It's not safe for y'all to travel that far without it."

"Got it right here," she replied, and displayed it for him to see. And then the Hunters—Meriwether, Phoebe, and even Abigail—glanced around their parlor one last time.

The '36 Chevy was packed so full, there was barely room in the back seat for Abigail, but she squeezed in and grinned.

"Likely we won't cross paths again anytime soon," Meriwether commented as he settled in behind the steering wheel. "Even though my wife and I still have family in Charleston, Michigan's quite a drive from Carolina."

"And cold with lotsa snow in the wintertime," Abigail said.

"Lotsa snow is something you know a lot about, right?" I reminded Meriwether.

"Sure thing. You remember the story, Gabriel. We had a lot of snow at the Battle of the Bulge."

"I remember, and you know what I hope?" I said.

"What's that, Gabriel?" Meriwether asked.

"That one day there'll be a parade for you and all the other colored heroes too."

He scanned the starry sky. "My heart wonders if that could ever be, but I'll hold on to your hope. After all, you were right about me havin' a car someday, weren't you?"

I chuckled. "Yessir, I was."

As he backed the car out of the driveway, everyone waved, and as it slowly disappeared into the darkness, I thought about what he'd taught me about seeing things more clearly when we look at them through more eyes than just our own. I stood there and imagined myself peering through Meriwether's eyes and realized he was heading off to what he hoped would be a better place with a better future. But through my eyes, I was losing a friend.

This allowed me to be happy and sad at the same time.

And that's why I was smiling when the tears came.

ACKNOWLEDGMENTS

FOR ALL OF the heroic men and women of color who admirably served in the United States Armed Forces during World War II, thank you. You will not be forgotten.

During a 2016 visit to the National WWII Museum in New Orleans, Louisiana, I was pleased to discover the inclusion of the numerous contributions made by African Americans who served heroically in the armed forces. Thank you.

Thank you to Nancy Paulsen for encouraging me to write this story, for her ongoing support, amazing instincts, and editorial skill. Thank you, Sara LaFleur, for all you do. Thank you to the copy editor, Laurel Robinson, and all the people at Penguin Random House who work hard to take the words of writers and create our books. A special thank-you to John Jay Cabuay for his amazing cover art.

As always, I acknowledge the Spirit's guidance.

Good humans come in all colors.

AFTERWORD

THE GREAT MIGRATION of African Americans out of the southern United States to the North and West during the 1940s and 1950s was prompted in part by the dissatisfaction of soldiers of color with the stifling oppression and cruelty of Jim Crow laws after their return from overseas. Some of these men even returned to take sanctuary in Europe. Many historians cite the maltreatment in the South of African American veterans who had served during World War II as one of the driving forces of the civil rights movement.

The 761st Tank Battalion was an African American United States Army unit that fought on the European front during World War II and saw action at the Battle of the Bulge. This group of brave men spent 183 days in continuous combat. Come Out Fighting was the motto chosen by these heroes. In 2005 a monument honoring the contributions made by this outstanding unit was finally erected at Fort Hood, Texas.

BIBLIOGRAPHY

The 761st "Black Panther" Tank Battalion in World War II: An Illustrated History of the First African American Armored Unit to See Combat, Joe W. Wilson, Jr. 1999. McFarland & Company, publishers.

BRENDA WOODS is an artist and a photographer, and she has a bachelor of science degree from California State University, Northridge. Her award-winning books for young readers include *The Blossoming Universe of Violet Diamond* (a CCBC Choice and a *Kirkus* Best Book), Coretta Scott King Honor winner *The Red Rose Box*, ALAN Pick *Saint Louis Armstrong Beach*, and *VOYA* Top Shelf Fiction selection *Emako Blue*. Her numerous awards and honors include the Judy Lopez Memorial Award, FOCAL Award, PEN Center USA Literary Award finalist, IRA Children's Choice Young Adult Fiction Award, and ALA Quick Pick. She lives in Nevada.